DRAGONS AND MORE

Dragon nature is the same the world over but no two dragons are alike. There are five in this collection of stories – from the menacing to the love-lorn – and other familiar fairy-tale figures show themselves equally vulnerable to the question life poses, both sad and comic, for every living creature. What does a polite King do when he finds he has a dragon neighbour? How can a pompous Mayor keep his dignity when a dragon trundles into town? What is the answer when a fox is too cowardly to make a kill? Or when a seagull, looking for freedom, comes across the largest bird-cage in the world?

DRAGONS AND MORE

Dark fables with some light patches

By

MILDRED DAVIDSON

Illustrated by
JOHN LAWRENCE

CHATTO & WINDUS · LONDON

Published by
Chatto & Windus Ltd
40–42 William IV Street
London WC2N 4DF

*

Clarke Irwin & Co. Ltd
Toronto

Text © Mildred Davidson 1976
Illustrations © John Lawrence 1976

ISBN 0 7011 5101 3

Printed in Great Britain by
Redwood Burn Limited
Trowbridge & Esher

CONTENTS

DRAGONS AND MORE

THE BROTHERS OF
THE GOLDEN HARVEST

It was young George who first let the Mayor of Cad know about the three strangers entering the town. Unfortunately young George, bright as he was, was only the general fetch-and-carry boy in the Mayor's kitchen. This meant that nobody listened to him. On this occasion, however, his story of the three men was so fantastic that everyone listened but no one believed him.

"The first man," young George said, "was gigantic, like a barrel in the middle, with. . ."

Then the Mayor who had a barrel of a middle himself snorted and said:

"Nonsense! The boy's telling fibs again."

Now George resented this not just because he happened to be truthful, but because the Mayor's bright-haired little daughter was listening.

"It's perfectly true," he said, deciding to stand up for his tale, "the first man had a dragon on a lead — like a dog — only it happened to be a dragon — a little one like this —" (he spread out his arms to show the size). "You couldn't mistake that it was a *dragon*!"

Yet if George's story made no impression on the Mayor, the alarm of the townspeople soon did. There was hardly time for the rumours to spread before the three men were marching boldly through the streets, moving like judgment towards the main square. In front of the first trundled the dragon, looking wickedly from side to side as the people vanished into buildings. How were they to know that it was only a baby dragon?

"Dragons!" they cried, multiplying George's account. "Great big fiery dragons!"

All the windows in the town were suddenly blinded.

11

Shutters came down and doors were barred. People mounted high up in their homes as if followed by a flood. The whole population looked down from upper storeys and held its breath.

Meanwhile the three men continued their march, heedless of the quaking town. The leader was a dull angry giant with legs like tree-trunks lifted from great roots and planted forcibly on the earth. His furious face burned round like the sun, his shadow was black as a chasm. On the edge of the blackness glided another, a thin, lurking, sneaking, spying fellow. Behind came a third man with a different face: a handsome youth who smiled at all the windows as he passed.

The procession arrived in the main square and approached the town hall. The Mayor, who was a fat little man as fond of his gold chain as he was of his golden-haired daughter, found that the people had left it to him to welcome this strange company. Harnessed in his chain, he was pushed out on the topmost balcony from where he eyed the giant and the dragon in turn. It was difficult to say which might prove the more dangerous.

"We are important persons," bellowed the giant, though a mere whisper coming from him would have been terrible enough. "Why aren't there people. . .people" — (he looked round at the empty square) — "to welcome us?"

"Wel-" said the Mayor, then he stopped, cleared his throat. "Welcome," he said nervously. There was a long pause. The Mayor couldn't manage another word.

"Welcome!" scoffed the stranger. "Welcome us with some food, before I set my dog on you." He shook the dragon's chain.

"Brothers," said the third man, smiling on three sides of his face, "I am sure these people intend to greet us most graciously." He turned to the Mayor. "Let it be a grand feast," he said, "with ladies and music. I am a lover of the fine life."

12

At once the Mayor and his household came to life. Never before was there such a fussing and a bustling, or so many joints sent up free of charge from the butcher, or so much bread from the baker. The best room in the town hall — the one with coats-of-arms in stained glass windows — was swept from ceiling to floor, chandeliers were lit, precious plate and ornaments were set out, and a large space cleared in one corner for the dragon.

Only the best people were invited to the feast. While it was being prepared they spent the time deciding what they should wear. First this and then that was taken up and set aside. Nothing seemed good enough, nothing could be too rich or too bright. Finally the ladies clasped on their jewels and bound up their locks with gold hairpins. The gentlemen dressed as if the King had arrived in Cad and graciously summoned them to dine. Everything was done to convince the strangers they were honoured guests — everything that bowing and scraping and the setting out of precious gold ornaments could do.

Only the common folk — souls too unimportant to be invited — remained hidden in upstairs rooms. Children were hushed and babies forbidden to cry. As for the dogs, it wasn't necessary to say anything to them, for they scented dragon and held their tongues.

Meanwhile the Mayor gave seats of honour to his three guests, while his little daughter helped with the serving. The servants of course were all frightened of the dragon, but he took quite readily to his corner and hardly seemed to mind that his food was tossed to him from a distance instead of being set down at close quarters.

"Are you travellers from far?" asked the Mayor, nervously plucking at his chain of office.

"Far enough," said the first man, attacking his food.

"Farther," murmured the second, shrinking and shrivelling beside his companion.

"We have travelled a long way," said the third, smiling

at the ladies, "and will be journeying back tomorrow."

"Will you?" said the Mayor, brightening up.

Relief spread through the room; the guests began to relax and the Mayor to puff himself out a little.

"I expect," he said, "that you come from a very fine dwelling and are anxious after your journey to be home again."

Number One gave number Three a wink.

"That's right," he said, "it's a very fine dwelling indeed."

"Magnificent," murmured number Two.

"Made of gold," said number Three.

"Gold!" gasped the Mayor.

"Gold!" cried all the guests.

"That's right," said the red-faced giant. "We thought it was time we did some repairs on it, so we've come to collect."

"Collect!" echoed the Mayor.

"Surely you have heard of us?" said the third stranger. "Here sits my magnificent brother Bellicose." (He pointed to number One who grunted loudly.) "Here is my clever brother Sly." (He touched number Two briefly but the man shrank from him.) "And I am known among men and women as Charm."

"Ah!" sighed the ladies.

"We three, Bellicose, Sly and Charm, are sometimes called the Brothers of the Golden Harvest. When we were born each of us was reared for fifteen years away from the light of the sun. So we learnt from our early youth to crave anything that shone gold. Now we surround ourselves with it. Any town that gains a reputation for its wealth can be sure to have a visit from us. Hearing that the town of Cad had a greedy Mayor and rich citizens, we thought it time to collect your gold and improve our dwelling. We have each of us a sack to fill before we leave in the morning."

"B. . .b. . .b. . .but we don't have any gold," cried the Mayor, clutching his chain.

14

"None at all," declared everyone present.

Bellicose snapped his fingers and a loud noise came from the corner. A puff of smoke helped to remind the people of the presence of the dragon.

"Here!" called Bellicose, and the dragon pranced forward with a wide sweep of his tail that caught one or two of the servants on the legs as they scattered before him. Only the Mayor's little daughter remained holding a dish behind Bellicose. The dragon seemed to entrance her.

"What pretty colours," she declared. The dragon turned a rather pleased eye in her direction.

"All right, all right," said the Mayor hurriedly. "We are poor people here, but you shall have the town's small supply of gold in the morning. I. . .I. . .take it you won't be returning."

"We never need to come twice," said Sly.

"Though we are rarely forgotten," said Charm.

"You won't be wanting *all* the gold?" tried the Mayor again, hopeful that it was a joke and plucking hard at his chain.

"Every scrap," said Bellicose heartily. "It will save a lot of time if you have it waiting for us in the morning. For whether you do or not, we shall certainly take it all."

The feast was finished. The Mayor stood on tip-toe to whisper to the tall butler. The butler murmured to the head-waiter so discreetly that none could tell his lips moved. The head-waiter twitched his face and all the serving-men and serving-women descended on the tables, stripping them of plate, cutlery, ornaments, candlesticks — all the precious items the Mayor had had put out on show. The three strangers settled down to sleep in front of the fire. The Mayor and his guests withdrew.

But not to sleep, indeed. There was too much to be done and very little time in which to do it. In the secret hours of the night the Mayor ordered half the town's gold to be collected and placed in the public square. The other half was

15

secretly locked away in cellars, together with the Mayor's gold chain and the gold plate used for the feast. There was much coming and going on back stairs, much soft padding from room to room and house to house until all was made as safe as locks and bolts could make it.

At break of day, Bellicose, Sly and Charm descended noisily to the courtyard. When he saw the array of gold, Bellicose laughed heartily.

"Come," he said, "let us see if it fits my sack."

From his pocket he drew a tightly folded piece of cloth, fine as silk but strong as the man himself. He shook it out and started piling in the gold set before him.

"See," he said when he got to the end, "it is only half full!"

Sure enough, the sack had swallowed up the gold like a miracle and still, before the people's astonished gaze, had room for more.

"Come brothers," said Bellicose, "we shall have to sniff it out."

"W. . .w. . .what d'you mean?" cried the Mayor. "You have all we can spare — absolutely all!"

But Bellicose merely remarked, looking round him for the dragon who seemed to have disappeared, "Where's that dratted animal gone? We shall need him to burn a few doors for us."

"W. . .w. . .wait," cried the Mayor again. "We must live. Have you not enough with *half* a sackful?"

"No," said Bellicose, "we do nothing by halves."

So the Mayor had the vaults opened and the town hall and the bank and the post office and all the buildings round about were made to disgorge their treasure.

"Almost full," said Bellicose heaving it into his sack. "What about that small store of your own, put by for a rainy day. I'll take that while I'm here."

The Mayor blushed. Everybody turned and looked at him. Small store indeed!

16

He drew himself up to his full height and was about to protest when the arrival of the dragon halted him. He gasped when he saw his daughter holding the lead and feeding the creature on buns of her own baking.

The Mayor gave in and allowed his own store of gold to be dug out from beneath the floorboards of his parlour.

"O-o-o-oh," gasped the people when they saw how much their Mayor had hidden. The Mayor, with a red face, pretended not to notice.

"Right," said Bellicose, "my sack is full. Your turn now brothers. I'll be on my way."

"Their turn!" said the people aghast.

"But you've got it all," cried the Mayor.

However, there was brother Sly shaking out his sack and pointing his skinny finger upwards to the gold weather vane that topped the town hall.

"Mercy on us," cried the Mayor, "that's part of the building!"

But down it came, and so did the gold-plated hands and numbers on the town-hall clock, leaving the face a featureless blank before the astonished crowd.

"Anything more you want, while I'm up here?" yelled down the workman who'd been sent skimming up the ladders on his day off and whose temper had not been improved on that account.

"That must be all," said the Mayor with a groan.

"The gold plate," murmured Sly, "the candlesticks, and the gold ornaments."

It was almost more than the people had heard him utter since he had arrived. It was evident that though Sly was the silent one nothing had escaped his attention.

"To think," muttered the Mayor, "he was weighing up what he would take from us while we were in the act of feasting him!"

Now, it seemed, all the town's riches were brought forth. Alas to be proud of your wealth and then to lose it.

The Mayor watched the sack filling up. Almost full. Yet still there was something lacking.

If the people's attention had not been fixed on other things, they might have noticed something different about the Mayor that morning. As it happened there was in the crowd a small boy whose attention was beginning to stray from Sly and Charm and the dragon.

"Oooh," he said, pointing at the Mayor. "That funny man's not wearing his chain."

There was a great laugh. It was perfectly true. The Mayor was not dressed as usual. He looked less pompous and considerably less important. He was in fact chainless. With tears of rage in his eyes, the Mayor now watched his chain of office popped into Sly's sack. Yet not even that filled it.

Now Sly's real ability came to light. He seemed to know just where each citizen had stored a little nest egg. He knew about those gold coins a wife had hidden from her husband and the spare piece of plate that a servant had pinched from his master. Then of course there was the tailor's gold tooth. With one motion of his hand Sly seemed to spirit it from the poor man's gaping mouth.

As he went from one person to another, they laughed, then cried, then grew angry. They began to shrink from Sly as he shrank from them.

At last the sack was full. Sly grinned at the remaining brother as he heaved it up and moved off. The Mayor and the people stared as Charm produced an empty sack. Was it possible there was anything left to put in it?

The debonair young man began his rounds with a bright smile. He took wedding rings first. Then the ladies' gold hairpins had been greatly admired by Charm the evening before, together with a great deal more jewellery. The men's little stock of gold signet rings, gold tie-pins, gold cuff-links and gold studs were of no mean value in a wealthy town like Cad. Then gold tassels on curtains and gold bars on bird-cages were all popped into the sack.

Nor did he forget the gold initials on the Mayor's under-clothing and the gold threads that ran through the ladies' garters, though one or two of the ladies fainted at this. It seemed that this charming young man would unresistedly take the last speck of gold-dust that shone in the town of Cad.

Now all was gathered up in Charm's sack. Nothing was left in the town that would gleam gold in the sunlight.

Stop! There was just one thing. Even Charm had over-looked one thing. He turned to where the dragon had settled contentedly at the feet of the Mayor's pretty daughter and was foolishly enjoying the way she tickled his chin. Her golden locks were brighter than the sun in a town that had lost all its gold.

Quickly Charm stepped up to her and produced from his pocket a silver comb. A brief flick through her hair, and there stood Charm with a comb that glittered gold in the sun, and there was the Mayor's little daughter with silver grey locks.

"No," cried the Mayor in real anguish. "Not my child! Not my darling little girl!"

But the business was over. Charm threw the comb into the sack. It would hold no more. After this last act he was in a hurry to be off. There was an astounded silence as Charm shouldered his burden and strode gaily on his way. No one wished him farewell. No one moved until he had gone.

Suddenly someone cried out:

"The dragon. What about the dragon?"

For there he still was, coiled contentedly round the feet of the Mayor's little daughter whose hair was now as grey as her grandmother's.

"They've left him behind," declared the Mayor. "We must get them to move him."

Someone ran along the street to see if he could catch up with Charm. He returned with the news that the three brothers had quitted the town as suddenly as they had come.

What was to be done? The dragon looked peaceful enough for he was indulging in a quiet nap, but even so, who dared approach him? Only the Mayor's daughter.

"My dear," said the Mayor, feeling slightly ridiculous, "you must get him to move. He must follow his master like a good (ahem!) dragon."

"Can't I keep him?" asked his daughter. "He's so lovely."

"No!" said the Mayor with decision, moving forward.

Just then the dragon opened one eye and gave a little puff of smoke out of one nostril. It was enough to send the crowd back several paces.

"You darling," said the Mayor's daughter, "you're tired. Go back to sleep."

Now an argument broke out.

"You can't keep him," said the Mayor desperately. "What are we to feed him on? We've no gold. And I suspect his favourite meal is human!"

Excited breathing from the dragon.

"He likes my buns," said the Mayor's daughter. "I'll bake for him every day. He shall have meat pie and apricot tart today."

The dragon gave her hand a little lick. But the look he turned on the crowd was amused and wicked.

Then that young general fetch-and-carry kitchen boy, who was devoted to the Mayor's little daughter, had an idea. He'd been thinking ever since Charm had closed his sack. Now he tore off down the street, out of the town, along the open road. There like specks against the open sky was the small procession. Three men were labouring in single file under heavy sacks.

George was used to running and running fast, for in Cad he had been at many a beck and call. The men had journeyed some distance but George didn't stop running until he had caught up with them.

"Whoa there," called Charm to Sly.

"Brother, there is news," called Sly to Bellicose.

They halted in turn and watched the young lad sprinting towards them.

"The dragon," panted George when he had sufficient breath to speak. "You've left the dragon behind."

"So we have," said Charm. "Brother, why isn't he with you?"

Bellicose had forgotten all about him.

"I'm not going back," he said. "I've got the heaviest load."

"We never go back," said Sly. "You know it's unlucky."

"We'll have to leave him then," said Charm.

"Ay, ay," said Bellicose. "He wasn't a very well trained creature and there's more where he came from. I say he's not worth bothering about. Let him stay where he is."

"What about us?" asked George. "We can't afford to feed him. You've got all our gold."

Bellicose laughed heartlessly. However, Charm said:

"We'll let you have one small piece, since you're going to keep the dragon for us."

"The smallest, mind!" said Sly jealously.

George glowed with excitement.

"All right," he said boldly. "We'll keep the dragon. And in return I'll take back the gold from the Mayor's daughter's hair."

Charm undid his sack and produced the shining comb.

"If you were to sell it in the right place," he said, "you might find it worth more than you think."

George took the precious comb with trembling hands, and carried it back to Cad as carefully as if he had been entrusted with the Crown jewels. He found the crowd still assembled in the square, and the dragon very much awake and frisky. He bore the comb proudly aloft and as the Mayor's daughter called her new pet to heel, he approached and drew the comb softly through her locks. The girl's hair shone once more with gold. Not a speck of it was lost. There remained in George's hand an unburnished comb.

Then George told the people what he had done, what bargain he had made, how he had promised they would keep the dragon and in return had received the golden hair.

The people were amazed, the Mayor was astounded at this new aspect of the poor fetch-and-carry boy. He had shown courage. But alas he had landed them with a dragon.

George pointed out that the dragon had had every intention of staying in any case.

Then perhaps. . .just perhaps. . .it would have been better for the town if he had brought back some of the gold money or gold plate (or, thought the Mayor, my gold chain!). But there was nothing the people could do about it. They could never again get the gold out of the girl's hair — the dragon would see to that. He quickly established himself as her bodyguard. The fame of the young lady spread far and wide, not just because of the dragon, but because she was the only *golden* thing in the town.

In future, when visitors came, they were no longer entertained with the gold candlesticks and the gold plate. The ladies no more donned their gold hairpins nor the gentlemen their gold cuff-links. Instead they were introduced to the Mayor's daughter as the town's shining treasure. The Mayor always said he placed great value on his golden-haired child — though his fingers continued to play idly with an invisible chain.

As for the dragon, he was devoted to the Mayor's daughter and usually behaved himself when she was at hand. For this reason it was considered safer for him to remain her constant companion. Meanwhile George went back to his kitchen and helped the Mayor's little daughter to bake dainties for the dragon. They got on famously in this way.

Yet George always had dreams of becoming much more

important. For he could see something that no one else in the town seemed to notice. The dragon was still only a baby — and big enough at that. One day he was going to grow into a larger dragon — a very much larger dragon!

"Perhaps," thought George, "that is where I shall come in."

But that is another story.

THE GIANT'S AXE

A long time ago there lived a Giant, a wicked, cunning, sly, vindictive, ugly Giant. He had a good sense of fun too. Wherever he went he took with him his axe, and had a habit of sweeping off people's heads whenever they crossed his path. This made them run when they saw him coming. So he ran too and because he could take such long strides, they rarely, if ever, escaped him. The Giant found it very good exercise.

When the heads were struck off by the axe, the people usually picked them up again and went away carrying them in their hands. But it wasn't the same thing as having your head placed firmly on your shoulders, and the people didn't like it a bit. Then to show what a stronge sense of fun he had, the Giant who was in the habit of sweeping off several heads in a matter of seconds, loved to tease the poor creatures afterwards by shifting the heads around a bit. So they often picked up the wrong heads and went off in utter confusion. The Giant had a good laugh.

Then the people got together and said to each other: "We must really do something about this Giant."

The next day they met again and said exactly the same thing.

The following day they came together and said: "We must really do something about this Giant."

The trouble was they had no idea what they could do.

One day the Giant raised his axe to strike off the head of a little tool-maker. While the Giant was giving a big swing to his weapon, the little tool-maker cried out, just in time: "What a blunt blade you have there, Giant."

The Giant paused in swinging the axe and stared at it.

"It doesn't look blunt to me," he boomed.

"Oh, I could make it much sharper for you," said the little tool-maker bravely. "You'd get a cleaner cut with it."

"Could you now?" said the Giant, obviously puzzled as to which would give him greater satisfaction — to sweep off the tool-maker's head or to have his axe nice and sharp. Then he thought that after all he could always cut off the tool-maker's head afterwards. The Giant laughed to himself at the thought, for he had a good sense of fun.

"All right," he said, "I'll let you have the axe and you can sharpen it for me."

So the little tool-maker took the axe home with him and sharpened the big blade on his grindstone, and sharpened it, and sharpened it, until the edge was one glancing stroke of light and keener than December frost. Then he said to himself:

"I'll just give the Giant a new handle to this blade while I'm about it."

So he got to work and fashioned a mighty handle for the keen steel. He made it big enough for a Giant and strong enough to strike off the head of an elephant at one blow. Then before he fitted the blade, he turned the handle round to the other side and notched the blade well into the back of the axe-handle, for both sides were like enough.

Then he carried the axe to the Giant who was really rather pleased when he saw the blade's cutting edge glinting in the sun.

"You can strike off seven heads at once with that razor," said the little tool-maker, proud of his work.

The Giant laughed, and to show his pleasure he whirled the axe high in the air, and brought it sweeping down to sever the little tool-maker's head from his body. But alas, the handle was heading in another direction. With the blade firmly notched in its socket the handle was moving backwards, towards the Giant. The force of his own blow carried off the Giant's head. The little tool-maker stood patiently by.

The Giant was quite confounded at this first experience of being beheaded. He had been spoilt by all his former success and he wasn't able to take his present defeat heroically. The tears coursed down the cheeks of the severed head, while the Giant's body lay on the ground flapping its arms and feet helplessly in the air.

"Come, come," said the little tool-maker kindly, "it happens to all of us some time, you know."

It was apparent it hadn't yet happened to him.

"Let me give you a helping hand," said the little tool-maker and he picked up the Giant's head, helped the Giant to his feet, and pressed the head into his hand.

The Giant went away miserably, his head emitting great howls of discomfort. There really wouldn't be any more trouble from him. But the people were very curious about the axe which he had carelessly left behind.

At first it was a curiosity and placed on show. But gradually it became so famous that many greedy people wanted to own it and quarrelled furiously over its possession. It was carried off all over the place, and stolen several times. But the people who were most successful in obtaining it by fair means or foul usually didn't keep their heads for very long, so it passed very quickly from one hand to the next.

At last it gained a reputation for wanting to decide its owner for itself. It was said that whoever could swing it without losing his head, would be the correct person to keep it. Many attempts were made to gain the axe's favour this way but the result was that even more people seemed to be carrying their heads in their hands.

The axe did so much business that it came back at last to the little tool-maker for sharpening. This time he thought he might have a go at winning possession of it. So he sharpened the blade as he had done before and polished the handle beautifully, only now he withdrew the blade from the back and slotted it into the other side. Then he swung the axe — only gently, for the steel was sparkling keen — and brought it straight down in front of him.

When the people saw that he could handle the axe and keep his head, they were forced to agree that the Giant's famous axe should be his. He used it many a time in his workshop, but later in life he put it on show in his home for the neighbours to come and look at. When he was very old it reminded him what a good workman he'd been.

The secret of the axe he told to no one.

THE UGLY PRINCE AND
THE UGLY PRINCESS

Once upon a time in the city of Throg there lived an ugly Princess. Not only was she ugly in appearance but she matched her ugliness by being sour and spiteful and angry. Now she happened to have a sister who was very beautiful and nothing made her more jealous or more spiteful than her beautiful sister.

As they grew up the beautiful Princess had many suitors for she was gentle and kind. The ugly Princess had none. It became clear to the Princesses' parents that they would have to arrange a husband for their ugly daughter.

Now the King of Habbaggug happened to have an ugly son as well as a handsome one. Both of them fell in love with the beautiful Princess of Throg who was gentle and kind. It was the handsome Prince who won her, but the King and Queen of Throg had the brilliant idea of marrying their ugly daughter to the ugly Prince as a kind of consolation prize.

"They will suit each other so well," they said. "Where else in the world could we find a Prince ugly enough to marry our ugly daughter?"

The ugly Prince himself, however, was not prepared to admit this. He wanted to marry a beautiful Princess, just as the ugly Princess wished to marry a handsome Prince. Both of them said:

"It isn't fair. . .and I won't. . .I won't. . .I won't!"

However, the King and Queen of Throg knew how to wheedle and coax and threaten. Finally there were no more suitors left because they had all gone home after the beautiful Princess married her handsome Prince. So the ugly Princess was persuaded to marry the ugly Prince and they quarrelled furiously all the time.

Neither would admit being married to the other, so they had a large palace built just on the border separating Throg from Habbaggug. The Princess lived in the half that lay in Throg and the Prince lived in the half that lay in Habbaggug. Their dining-table was placed exactly midway, so that the Princess could sit on one side and the Prince could sit on the other and both could eat in their own domain. So this foolish state of affairs continued for a long time.

Then one day the Princess said aloud:

"Surely there is some way to rid me of this ugly husband. I storm and rage when I think what a toad I am married to."

A page-boy heard her say this and chirped aloud:

"Why doesn't the Princess consult the old witch of Throg? She can do anything if she has a will to it."

"Who said that?" demanded the Princess who wasn't in the habit of noticing page-boys.

"I did," chirped the voice.

The Princess was forced to bend her head and take note of the lad.

"Tell me more," she said, "for a Princess cannot be expected to know where a witch lives."

"I'll show you," said the boy promptly. "It will be better to go at midnight as that's her hour for seeing visitors."

So the Princess stepped out at midnight to visit the old witch of Throg.

"Come in, ugly Princess," called the witch, "and tell me what you want."

The Princess was not pleased at being called ugly, but she knew that witches cannot be expected to obey the laws and customs of ordinary mortals. So she twitched her robes around her and entered. The witch was not, perhaps, quite as ugly as the Princess.

"I see," said the witch with a cackle when the Princess had explained her visit. "You want me to rid you of your husband because he's ugly. Well, well, that is very amusing to be sure. It is as sweet to me as a maggot in an apple. Such a good joke mustn't be allowed to fail. I'll help you with all my heart."

Meanwhile the Prince was saying at the palace:

"If only I could rid myself of this ugly wife, how much happier I should be. No one will come near us because she is so ugly."

Then the voice of a servant boy was heard.

"Why doesn't the Prince visit the wise wizard of Hab-baggug? He would help him do anything he wanted."

"The boy's right," said the Prince, greatly struck. "The wizard will be sure to understand my plight. I'll visit him before dawn."

So the Prince set out to call on the wizard.

Now the wizard was greatly amused by the Prince's situation and promised to help. He flew off to the palace immediately to view his task. At that very same moment the old witch of Throg arrived to spy out the land. These two hadn't seen each other for a long time and when they came face to face their backs bristled.

"You're on my ground, wizard," called the witch. "This palace is mine and all in it."

"There's half of it in Habbaggug," said the wizard. "What are you doing so close to my territory?"

"None of your business," declared the witch.

"Well," said the wizard, "if it has to do with an ugly Princess then it is my business."

"Wrong!" shouted the witch. "It has to do with an ugly Prince."

The two of them brought their great noses together and growled and whistled.

"Toothless one!" grunted the wizard.

"Witless!" shrieked the witch.

"We'll see about that," called the wizard.

Now the witch had begun to think that she might stand

more chance in this struggle if she enlisted the aid of her old friend, the Giant of the East. Like a shot she was off, leaving the wizard threshing at the empty air.

The Giant of the East's dwelling was surrounded by thorny-sharp stones. Whoever approached him must first cross these and therefore it was usually only workers of magic who visited him. The old witch of Throg came barely up to the Giant's knee when they stood together, so great in size was he. So she raised herself up on a little cloud and hung suspended before his face.

"What can I do for you?" he boomed loudly.

"I want your help," said she, "against a mean, skinny, spiteful old scoundrel who calls himself the wizard of Habbaggug."

"That should be easy enough," said the Giant. "He is a weed I shall tear from the ground between two fingers."

"Beware his tricks," said the witch, holding on hard, "for he is wily enough to enlist the aid of the Giant of the West."

The Giant's brow grew so crinkled that the witch felt she could hide between the ridges, and his teeth ground together as if all the stones round his dwelling were at one and the same time sharpening their points.

Meanwhile the wizard of Habbaggug had indeed taken it into his head to visit the Giant of the West, who lived in a land of slippery dunes constantly moving and changing shape and therefore not usually visited by mortal men.

"I want your help," the wizard told him, "against an adder-bitten poisonous old witch. I suspect that she is plotting with the Giant of the East."

"What, that stormy creature!" cried the Giant of the West. "There will be battle royal today."

There was a sound of all the hills running together like soldiers into ranks, preparing to march forth. But the Giant of the West knew that he and his great enemy were too well matched to make it an easy battle, so he thought that first he would seek an ally in the West Wind.

So the Giant stalked off with long strides as far west as it was possible to go. There he found caves that dwarfed even his great bulk, and gusts of wind filling them. A great sighing came from one cave. Then with a rush of air that nearly bowled the Giant over, a voice said:

"What can I do oo oo oo o for you oo oo o?"

The Giant grasped hold of a rock to steady himself and bellowed back:

"Lend me your strength against the Giant of the East. Ride eastwards and help me to destroy him."

More sighs came from the cave.

"I will," they whispered resoundingly one after the other. "When you have departed I shall come forth and ride the sky."

Then the Giant made a hasty escape for he knew he would never survive an encounter with the full force of the West Wind.

Meanwhile the Giant of the East strode gloomily to the caverns of the sharp East Wind, high up on a dismal plateau, and shouted loudly to him:

"We are two of a kind, you and I."

The East Wind's cries pierced him with cold.

"Come with me into battle," called the Giant.

"I will," shrieked the wind.

Then people on earth saw a terrible sight. In the east large storm clouds shrouded the heavens. In the west the sky was black. The winds rushed towards each other at full speed, yelling a battle cry as they went. The great Giants of East and West hurried to their homes to hide until the fury had passed.

The winds met at last with a great shock and grappled with each other, right above the palace built by the ugly Prince and the ugly Princess. The building shook so much that the ugly Princess was thrown right out of bed and catapulted from Throg into Habbaggug, into the arms of the ugly Prince. They clung together for protection against the wild storm. The building creaked and groaned. The timbers heaved. The roof began to cave in.

"Help me, Prince," called the Princess. "Help me. . .help me. . .handsome Prince!"

Lo and behold, a great change was taking place.

"I shall protect you with my life, beautiful Princess," he answered.

The winds ceased, the giants drew back, the witch of Throg and the wizard of Habbaggug were parted by a magic stronger than their own. In all the years that followed nobody ever heard any quarrel between the beautiful ugly Princess and the handsome ugly Prince.

THE KING'S NEIGHBOURS

"My dear," said the King looking out of the window one day, "we have neighbours."

"Good gracious," said the Queen, "that hasn't happened for a long time."

"It's happened now," said the King, "just as I said it would. If everyone else has neighbours I don't see why we shouldn't, just because we're royal."

"Quite right, my love," said the Queen.

"I think we must visit them," said the King.

"You are the pink of courtesy," said the Queen. "Go first and tell me what they're like. You know how long it takes me to put on the royal robes."

So the King who was both pink and courteous set out to call on his left-hand neighbour. This was a miser who had built himself a very high tower and thrown round it seven ramparts and seven ditches, in order to protect his wealth.

When the King got to the first rampart and the first ditch he found his way barred. Looking round, he spied a tiny metal tube coming out of the ground near the gate. The King bent down to the tube and finding it very dusty he blew into it. There was a strange noise from a long way off, as if someone at the end of the tube had had the dust blown in his ear.

"Hallo," said the King looking into the tube.

"What do you want?" came a voice back from it.

The King was delighted and pretended it was the most usual thing in the world to speak to a tube.

"Well," he called back, "I'm the King, your neighbour. I thought you might give me the pleasure of welcoming you. The trouble is I've come to a bit of a barrier."

"You're after my money," said the voice suspiciously.

41

"Oh dear me, no!" said the King in genuine surprise. "I've plenty of that. At least I think I have. The Lord Treasurer looks after these things and he says —"

"Have you got it with you?" asked the voice.

"I'm afraid not," said the King. "I never carry it anywhere. The Lord Treasurer always insists on doing that for me, or else he gets someone else to do it. I really don't know how far down the line money goes. I was always told I was several stages above it."

"I can't admit you," said the tube directly, "if you've no money with you. I like to look at it, you see."

"Oh I do see, quite," said the King politely, rarely bothering to look at money himself. "Still it's a pity that we shouldn't meet. The Queen was so looking forward to having neighbours. Suppose I get her to put on the Crown jewels — they're more precious than all the money and so pretty."

"Done!" said the voice.

So the King hurried off home and said to the Queen:

"Such a nice neighbour we have, my dear. But he wouldn't let me in unless you came too. I promised him that you would dress in all your jewellery and look just like a Queen."

The Queen was delighted to have the opportunity of wearing her jewels, though to put on all the royal rubies, sapphires, diamonds, emeralds, and pearls at once was no easy task. She adorned herself with as many rings, bracelets, necklaces, brooches, and coronets as she could safely fit on to her person. The weight of it was dreadful but she didn't mind, for she saw the visit as a royal duty.

"Come, my dear," said the King, leading her perilously forth, swaying in glory. "This way if you please."

They had to walk very slowly because of the heaviness of the Queen's jewellery, but when they reached the outer rampart of the miser's home the King bent down to the speaking-tube and said that he had arrived with the Queen who had arrived with the jewels. Then bridges were lowered for them, seven times over, until they reached the high tower that was the miser's dwelling.

The miser himself came toddling out of the low round cavern that formed the mouth of the tower. His thin arms hugged his thin chest for very greed, and his knees knocked suspiciously against each other.

"This way," he called in his wizened voice, hardly able to take his wizened eyes off the bejewelled Queen.

Then he led them through the hole that was the mouth of the tower and downwards through long rusty tunnels and through several more holes and gaps until they reached his central room. The King was wondering all the time why they didn't mount the tower.

"A regular warren," said the miser gleefully in his rusty voice. "It's very cosy you see, underground."

"It is certainly very warm," panted the Queen.

"I thought I noticed a tower —" said the King.

"It's a look-out," the miser told him. "It misleads any enemy who comes searching for my riches. They'll have a long way to travel before they find them. Especially if they go up the tower. He, he!"

"Do you think, dear," gasped the Queen, "that you could help me off with some of these ornaments?"

"Let me, let me," cried the miser with all the eagerness his shrivelled form could muster. "Your majesty must make yourself at home."

When the man had whipped off the Queen's rubies and sapphires and diamonds and emeralds and pearls, and she had sighed with relief, their host produced two thimblefuls of water for his guests to drink.

"Whatever is that noise?" asked the King, for there were light little hammer blows on the surface above their heads.

"That's the rain," said the miser. "Dear me, it must be heavy. I don't usually hear it down here."

"However shall we get home?" exclaimed the Queen.

"The royal robes will be quite spoilt. And the Crown jewels will get wet."

"Ah," said the miser, rubbing his hands. "I have just the plan. You need not go out of doors at all until you get to your own gate. My underground passages stretch very far. Right under the ramparts and the ditches, although no one knows it, and there's a special entrance quite close to your own palace."

"How wonderful," cried the Queen.

"Only," said the miser cunningly, "it would be much too narrow and much too warm for your majesty to wear your jewels. I suggest you leave them with me and send for them tomorrow. They'll be more than safe here, I promise you."

The Queen was only too glad to take the miser's advice, and with many thanks on their part and many gratified wheezes on their host's, the King and Queen were escorted along and around and through and finally upwards as the passages led from the heart of the miser's dwelling to the outer gate of the palace.

"Good gracious," said the Queen, blinking as she came up into daylight.

Before she and the King could turn to say farewell, their neighbour had popped out of sight and the ground had closed firmly behind him.

"Tomorrow, my dear," said the King, "we must call on our other friend. Perhaps we shall have success there too."

The next morning the King went off alone to call on his second neighbour because it was taking the Queen such a long time to put on the royal robes after the labours of the day before. He took the right-hand path from the palace and came to a very draughty-looking castle. He pulled the bell rope and heard the slow clip-clop of the ancient porter coming on stiff legs. Suddenly there was a great rushing noise and smoke issued through the cracks at the sides of the gates.

"Good gracious," said the King as the portals swung open and there behind the gnarled old porter stood — a dragon.

"This is the dwelling of Lord Gnash-fast," warbled the porter in his high old voice, well-rehearsed beforehand.

"That's me," declared the dragon too eager to wait longer. "It's an old title of mine."

"Really," said the King, trying to pretend he wasn't talking to a dragon. "I'd no idea I had such a distinguished neighbour."

"Haaaaaaaaaah!" breathed the dragon, puffing out more smoke and giving his lips a little lick. "You'd better come in. Quick with you."

The King made all speed when bidden, assuming that the dragon's sounds indicated hospitality. He soon discovered that the dragon was a very sudden creature. He created most of the draughts in the castle by rushing down the corridors at great speed. He had bounded up to the gate before the porter could reach it when he heard the bell being pulled. Now he darted ahead of his guest and darted back again. Such sudden movements could only declare that he was a very discontented creature.

Now in his time the dragon had been ambitious — very ambitious indeed. He thought he would become famous if he frightened Kings into giving him their daughters, with the purpose of making these pretty maidens his own hand-maids; they would wait on him all day, they would serve him wine when he became fiery and dance when he wanted entertaining, they would rub his head with linseed oil, they would decorate his rose gardens with their beauty and his name would sound throughout the land. Well, it was true he had been successful in cowing a good many Kings in his time; he had always refused the money they offered and insisted on carrying off their daughters. There were fifteen of them mewed up in his castle at the present moment.

Only there are some of us for whom things never seem to turn out absolutely the way we expect them to. Lord

Gnash-fast was one of these unfortunates. He had always done things suddenly without thinking much about them beforehand. For instance he had never thought — not even on the fifteenth occasion — of inspecting a princess before refusing the gold in her place. It had never occurred to him that princesses are sometimes as ugly and as plain as other people. It had never occurred to him that instead of fifteen pretty waiting-maidens he would end up with fifteen frights. But so it was. One princess squinted, one was skin and bone, one was short and stumpy, one was horsey and one had a pug nose. The prettiest of the lot had been so spoilt that her face was constantly twisted with a dislike of this and a dislike of that. The dragon turned them all into drudges, making them hide their faces from him by having them kneel and scrub floors all day.

So as Lord Gnash-fast grew older, his temper had not improved.

Now he breathed very fast as he rushed the King into a huge armchair and asked:

"Have you a daughter?"

"Well, now," said the King, "as it happens, I have. The dearest, sweetest, prettiest creature imaginable. Do *you* have a daughter, Lord Gnash-fast?"

The dragon who had never been asked this question before was thrown slightly off course.

"No!" he barked shortly.

Then reducing his voice to a pathetic little whine, he played an old dragon's trick.

"It's because I haven't one of my own, that I asked after yours," he said. "Is she a good girl? Is she a kind girl?"

"Oh yes," answered the King.

"My eyes are growing dim these days. I wondered if you would spare her to read to me for a few hours. Age is so distressing."

The dragon crinkled the skin under his eyes until they almost disappeared.

46

"To be sure she will read to you," said the King. "The Queen and I have been wishing for neighbours for such a long time that any request of yours must be granted. I'll go straight home and collect her."

"Do!" said the dragon rising suddenly and trying to force his guest to greater speed.

So the King hurried home and told the Queen that he had promised their daughter should go and read to Lord Gnash-fast.

"We must receive him at court," said the Queen, "since he is a distinguished Lord."

"Certainly, my dear," said the King. "But I'll just take the Princess along to him now."

So the King carried off his daughter to the draughty-looking castle of Lord Gnash-fast and when he had pulled at the bell, he heard the dragon rushing towards the gate. It was flung open in a cloud of smoke.

"Here's my daughter come to read to you," said the King beaming. The dragon gazed out at the King and then dropped his eyes down and down and down — to the little girl that stood by the King's side.

The little Princess looked up at the huge creature and said:

"Whatever are you?"

The dragon was almost paralysed when he realised that the beautiful Princess was a little girl, but he managed to stutter after a few moments:

"A dragon!"

"My governess is a dragon and you don't look one bit like her."

"My dear," said the King, "you shouldn't notice these things. Would you like to stay and read to Lord Gnash-fast?"

"If he is intelligent enough to listen," said the Princess. Then she explained to the dragon: "My governess is always saying you have to be intelligent to listen properly."

"I'm sure," said the King to the dragon, "that you will

47

enjoy her company. Send her home when she has read enough."

The dragon was choked to the brim with a speechless rage. When he was alone with the Princess in his draughty castle, she asked him directly:

"Is something the matter with you?"

"I – thought – of meeting – a pretty – Princess," panted the dragon.

"But I am pretty," she said. "Especially in this new sash. It matches the colour of my eyes. Only you have to wear a sash round your waist you know."

The dragon looked down at the small face and it was true – she wasn't all that bad-looking – for a little girl.

"I – thought – you'd be – older," he managed again.

"I shall become older."

"That's not the same thing," he said. "I don't like waiting."

"I often pretend I'm older."

"That won't do either. I don't like pretending."

"You're very funny," she said. "Not one bit like a dragon. Not a bit like my governess I mean. Shall I read to you?"

She hopped quickly up on to the dragon's knee.

Meanwhile back at the palace the Lord Chancellor was announcing to the King a Grand Occasion.

"Next month," he said, "there will occur your majesties' wedding anniversary, and all the usual guests have been invited. I have the list here –"

He started to unwind the scroll.

"You will see that the Emperor is sending his sister and two of his sons to attend the Occasion, and that apart from eight Kings and Queens, we shall have no fewer than twenty-four Princes and Princesses, a hundred and twenty ambassadors and five hundred and seventy lords, ladies and gentlefolk. In addition, of course, the Duke Crusty-field."

The Queen wrinkled her royal nose. She didn't like the King's uncle, the old Duke Crusty-field. He was always so outspoken.

"It's dreadful how he never misses a single Occasion," she sighed.

"It sounds very satisfactory," said the King who was always worried by Grand Occasions.

"May I remind your majesty that it will be an Occasion," said the Lord Chancellor, "for the Crown jewels. The Princess too will have to be present this year. I suggest we start rehearsing our parts right away."

"Oh, ah!" said the King. "It might be a little early for that. The Crown jewels and the Princess are both out on loan at the moment."

"On loan, your majesty!" exclaimed the Lord Chancellor who never acted even in his off-moments as anything other than the Lord Chancellor. The King sighed. He hated explaining things.

When the Lord Chancellor heard that one neighbour had in his possession the Crown jewels and the other neighbour had the Princess, he was very quiet. Neither the King nor the Queen liked it when the Lord Chancellor was very quiet.

The Lord Treasurer had to be told, of course, and the Princess's governess.

"The jewels with a miser!" said the Lord Treasurer.

"The Princess with a dragon!" said the governess.

"I shall go myself," announced the Lord Chancellor, "AND PUT THINGS RIGHT!"

So the Lord Chancellor took his staff of office in his hand and went first to visit the miser. A very impressive man he was, with a very impressive walk and a very impressive frown. He discovered, however, when he got to the miser's home and was faced by the first rampart, that there was no one in sight to be impressed by him. He knocked at the gate but nothing happened.

49

"Ahoy there, my man!" he called.

A few wheezes appeared to be coming from the ground. The Lord Chancellor looked round but so bulky was he, and so used to keeping his head in the air, that he hardly spied the little bit of tube that poked up from the earth. It had to wheeze very badly before he took any notice of it.

"I'm not going to speak to a tube," said the Lord Chancellor disdainfully.

Then he waited and waited. After a while a head peered down at him from over the wall.

"What are you wanting?" called the miser.

Then the Lord Chancellor replied with all the dignity of his office:

"I demand the return of the Crown jewels — on pain of death."

"He, he!" said the miser. "I can tell you're not a King. You've not got the manners. Go back to your master and tell him I'm keeping the jewels warm for him. They're all right with me. No one's going to get their hands on them — least of all you!"

Then the miser popped down from the wall and the Lord Chancellor was left to swallow his defeat.

He next took his staff of office and went to call on Lord Gnash-fast. The dragon for once did not bound up to the gate when the bell was sounded. He had the Princess on his knee and she was reading to him from a big book that he felt obliged to hold for her. So immersed had he become in the story that he no longer cared to be the first to greet his visitors.

So it was that the Lord Chancellor was admitted to the castle and to the dragon's private study where the reading was going ahead. Then — and only then — did the dragon become like his old self. His head came up with spectacles perched on his nose, and a little smoke issued from his nostrils.

"Ugh," said the Princess, "I don't like smoke."

50

"Sorry, my dear," said the dragon, swallowing it bravely for her sake, and trying instead to "Grrrrrrrrr" at his guest.

"I have come for the Princess," said the Lord Chancellor loftily. "Please to hand her over, on pain of death."

"You threaten me!" cried the dragon enraged.

The Princess said:

"Don't be silly. The Lord Chancellor always talks like that. It doesn't mean anything. You should meet my governess and then you'd know!"

"I shall keep the Princess as long as I please," said the dragon.

He wished he could get up and confront the Lord Chancellor face to face, but it was impossible with the Princess on his knee.

"Old and blind dragon," said the Lord Chancellor, well puffed out now, and thinking he had the dragon's measure, "I demand the Princess."

Since the Princess was beginning to be scorched by the dragon's fire, she obligingly hopped off his knee and went to the Lord Chancellor.

"Why have you come for me, please? Is there some special reason?"

"You will be needed," said the Lord Chancellor, "for the Grand Occasion next month. You must rehearse your part and be dressed for it. We need both you and the Crown jewels, and it seems that the King your father has parted with you to one neighbour and with the jewels to another. It will be a miracle if we get the jewels back at all."

"Lord Gnash-fast must come to court for the Grand Occasion," said the Princess, now surrounded by smoke. "Come out from there, Lord Gnash-fast, and tell me you will be our guest. The Chancellor will add you to the list."

Then confidingly she whispered to the Chancellor: "I think you'd better."

So the Lord Chancellor brought out his list and added

Lord Gnash-fast's name, saying — "By request of the Princess."

The smoke began to subside.

As the days passed the little Princess went to and fro between the dragon's dwelling and the palace. First she learnt her part for the Grand Occasion and then she rehearsed Lord Gnash-fast in his.

One day she told him:

"The Lord Treasurer says that the Grand Occasion can't be held without the Crown jewels. My father left them with a miser who never answers when people visit him. No one can reach his home because he has seven ramparts and seven ditches. My father says we needn't worry about the safety of the jewels. Only it would be nice to have them for the Grand Occasion. Otherwise it won't happen, you see. Then everyone will say that the King and Queen don't have a wedding anniversary any more. And unless we get the jewels back there won't be any more Grand Occasions at all."

Lord Gnash-fast breathed very hard and his eyes grew red.

"*I* shall settle this miser," he said.

With that he charged forth and in several bounds had passed the King's palace. When he came to the seven ramparts and seven ditches he called out:

"What a miserable toad it is that needs such protection for his skinny legs!"

There was no reply to this, so the dragon marched backwards and forwards singing loud dragon songs. This went on all day and right through the night. Eventually a piece of tube pushed up from the ground and waved perilously in front of the dragon's face. Then a very shaky voice came out of it.

"Go away!"

"Not without the jewels," declared the dragon.

"Have you money to pay for them? They're very expensive."

Now the dragon was rash when it came to declaring his gains. He called out:

"All the money in the world."

"Very well," said the miser, who was tired of having this fiery creature roaring outside his gates. "Bring it here. If you can make a pile of gold three feet high and six feet square, I'll exchange it for the jewels."

The dragon zoomed back to his castle. He had not a fraction of such gold, but he knew one way of getting it. In fact, he thought, it might give him some satisfaction in the process. He called for the fifteen Princesses who had been sweeping and cleaning and washing his castle for him and one by one he carried them homewards — each to the particular kingdom he had snatched her from.

"All right," he called, "I'll take payment in gold and you can have your daughter back."

One by one the delighted Kings took back their ugly daughters and willingly gave the dragon his gold pieces in their place.

Meanwhile, Lord Gnash-fast was beginning to feel another dragon entirely. A much cleaner dragon, a creature of heart as well as spirit.

When he had surrendered the last of the Princesses and had gathered in return a huge pile of gold, he carried it on to neutral territory, just outside the King's palace, and the little Princess helped him to measure out a square of six feet. Then they piled the gold up three feet high. After this the dragon went to the miser's dwelling and roared aloud for him to come forth.

He waited a long time but nothing happened.

"Over here," cried the Princess from beside the gold. The dragon bounded back to his treasure and there at last he heard the miser's voice, coming as it were from the midst of it.

"Let me out, will you. How can I get through my door
with such a weight on it?"

The dragon looked bewildered, but the little Princess
said:

"He's trying to come up out of the ground."

"Of course I am," called the miser. "You don't suppose
I use the front gates with all those ditches and ramparts, do
you?"

The dragon heaved up the gold once more and moved it
to another plot of ground. Then the miser's head popped
up from his secret door and he glanced hurriedly to see
that the gold was in order.

"Don't forget the jewels," called the dragon.

"I'll bring them," said the miser. "Just give me time.
You can't expect such speed from an old man like me.
You can see my legs are shaking already."

Actually the sight of gold always had this effect on the
miser, causing him to tremble violently at the mere prospect of possessing it.

They were forced to wait until he came and went — up
and down through his trap-door — bringing the jewels piece
by piece.

"You're such a fierce beast," he said to the dragon —
whose eyes were very red and glinting at that moment
— "that I don't know I can trust you. When I've brought
all the jewels up you might take advantage of an old man
like me and carry them off and the gold as well."

"No, he won't," promised the Princess. "Though the
jewels weren't yours to bargain over in the first place."

"That's what I'm thinking," said Lord Gnash-fast carelessly.

At this point the King looked out of the palace window,
then turned excitedly to the Queen.

"Do you know, my dear, both our neighbours are on
our front lawn getting to know each other. Do you think

we should take some tea out and join them? It's such a fine day."

"Of course, my love," said the Queen. "I always say you are the pink of courtesy."

So the King and Queen graciously went out, followed by a butler carrying an urn and a butler carrying the cups and saucers and a maid carrying the bread, butter and jam, and another maid carrying the cakes. They marched right up to where the miser was arguing with Lord Gnash-fast.

"How delighted the Queen and I are," said the King, beaming, "to see our two friends enjoying each other's company. We shall have tea all together here on the lawn."

The dragon and the miser were halted right in the middle of their debate. Around them lay gold and jewels in profusion, but there was the Queen taking her place behind the urn and pouring each a cup of tea, and there was the King gallantly carrying round the bread and butter — so anxious were both to wait upon their neighbours.

"Such a comfort on a warm afternoon to have a picnic on the lawn," said the King. "We are so pleased you could come."

The dragon bolted a whole plateful of bread and butter without thinking, whereas the miser could hardly eat anything for casting an eye over his precious gold. Then the little Princess clapped her hands and exclaimed:

"How nice it all is."

"Why, my dear," said the Queen at last, "our friend must have been in the process of returning the Crown jewels. Isn't that my ruby coronet over there in the grass? And the bracelets I see sparkling in the sun? So kind of him to bring them himself!"

"Ahhhhhhhhhh!" sighed the miser.

"We'll get the butler to carry them in," said the King. "You mustn't tax your strength further. Stay and have another cup of tea."

"No," cried the miser frantically.

"Yes, yes, of course you must," said the Queen kindly. "The jewels are very heavy for a man of your years to carry so far."

When tea was over, the King and Queen invited both the miser and Lord Gnash-fast to attend the Grand Occasion, and the Crown jewels were borne back into the castle with many cries of gratitude on the Queen's part and many groans on the miser's.

Then when the royal party was over the dragon scooped up a pile of gold and said:

"You won't be needing this, will you?"

"Stop!" cried the miser. "That's my gold you're taking."

"Oh no," said the dragon. "You haven't kept your part of the bargain. You don't have any jewels to give me, do you? So I don't see any reason to keep mine."

"Wait, wait," cried the miser, "we're neighbours aren't we?"

At which the dragon emitted a huge roar. The miser thought it was anger and fled without more ado into his hole in the ground. But the Princess could have sworn it was laughter.

At any rate, Lord Gnash-fast attended the Grand Occasion in a very expensive suit and the Princess was very proud of her friend who aroused considerable curiosity among the other guests at court. They were of course much too polite to comment on his unusual looks. All, that is, except old Duke Crusty-field. He fulfilled the Queen's worst fears. He went up to Lord Gnash-fast and peered curiously at him through each eye-glass in turn.

"Bless my soul," he declared in astonishment, "you're actually a *dragon*! I always knew they were mad here."

The miser, on the other hand, did not emerge from his underground warren for the Grand Occasion. It might have been that he was otherwise employed, digging further afield. Possibly — by accident, of course — through to Lord Gnash-fast's castle. Even perhaps to the special room in which Lord Gnash-fast kept a pile of gold. Still, Lord Gnash-fast would hardly care about these things, being a greatly reformed dragon.

THE FIGHTING MAN

The sun was sitting atilt on the most beautiful of blue skies. Clip clop! Clip clop! A knight was on his way to battle, his horse merrily turning up its silver hooves as they clopped over cobbles, then clumped over the grassy fields, past a simple farm where an old woman was sitting in the sun.

"Good day to you, old woman," called the knight. "It is good to rest in old age."

"I have three sons," called back the old woman. "They do the work and leave me in peace."

"It is good to be at peace in old age," returned the knight.

The old woman nodded and nodded in the sun.

"You are armed for battle," she said, squinting at him.

"Yes," said the knight. "I am on my way to fight in a noble cause and I shall gain great glory if I conquer in single combat the Knight of the Black Plume. He is a powerful demon who has never yet been overcome. I hope to be the knight of all knights who will lay him in the dust."

The old woman nodded as if she had only half heard so the knight nodded back and rode on his way.

Clip clop! Clip clop! Down through the woods towards the clearing, through the narrowing trees and into the bright green field. There rode the Knight of the Black Plume disguised from head to toe in his trappings. Like peacocks plumed for courtship the knights reared at one another.

There followed the clashing of armour, the pounding of hooves, the thrust of lances. Three times the knight turned and turned about in the noble cause. At the third advance the Knight of the Black Plume fell and the news carried as swiftly as birds could fly, spreading the glory of the victor far and wide.

Now the knight rode home, his horse half-blinded, his armour dinted, but with his heart high. As he retraced his steps he passed once more the old woman's cottage. He found her no longer sitting in the sun but labouring slowly under a heavy sack.

"What have you there, good woman," he called. "What have you so important in your sack that your son cannot carry it for you?"

"There is grain in my sack," replied the old woman as she bent nearly double under the weight, "and my eldest son lies within resting."

"Resting!" cried the knight. "How can he rest while his mother works? He will never win the glory I have won this day. Have you not heard how I killed the Knight of the Black Plume and stripped him of all his finery? Behold the plume itself decking my horse's ears."

The old woman raised her eyes to the knight.

"My son lies within, dead," she said, and bent again beneath her load.

"Dead!" echoed the knight aghast. "Truly, that is a misfortune when he was so young and you are so old. How did he come to die, old woman?"

"There was an accident," mumbled the old woman into the dust. "At the mill a sack of grain tumbled from its ledge. The blow destroyed him."

"A sad loss," murmured the knight. He was moving on when a thought struck him and he turned back to the woman. "Give me your blessing, old woman, in my hour of glory. They say it is lucky to have a fair wish from the first old crone one meets after a fight."

The woman looked up again at him and her eyes looked into him and through him.

"So that you may enjoy your fame to its utmost," she said, "may you take a long time in growing old."

"That's as fair a wish as may be," laughed the knight and proceeded on his way.

Four hundred years went by before the same man passed the same cottage.

"Ahoy there, old woman," called the soldier, "are you still there? I am on my way to join the King's battle along with many others, and for this I shall have a full purse before the day is over."

"You fight in a different cause this time," croaked the old crone.

"Indeed I do," said the soldier. "I couldn't afford this cockade or leather jerkin without the cash. Nowadays I fight here and I fight there according to which side pays the highest price. A man in his prime likes his luxuries and fighting pays for them. Besides, this time we fight a rich enemy and there should be a fine booty. I might bring you a purse or two when I ride home again."

The old woman just shook her head and the soldier spurred his solid horse forward.

That day there was a fierce and noisy battle when the plain rang with the shouts of the victors and the groans of the vanquished. The soldier rode out from the smoke of the cannon with his saddle laden with plunder.

As he passed again the old woman's farm he saw her this time drawing heavy buckets of water from the well.

"Ahoy, old woman," said the soldier boldly, "you will grow old indeed in that occupation. Have you not two sons left to do that work for you?"

"My second son," said the old woman, "was today drowned in the rising waters of the river. He was the one who always drew water for our house. Now it is I who do it."

And with these simple words she resumed her task.

"Truly," said the soldier, "there are some in the world who win the fight and some who lose. It appears that I am a winner and you are a loser. If your son had won the riches that I have gained this day, you would not be labouring in this manner now. Still, I have fought hard and it is my due."

He patted his saddlebags and rode on his way.

After another four hundred years the man again passed the old woman's cottage. He was on foot this time and dressed more plainly than before in a dull khaki suit. When the old crone saw his steel helmet rise just above her hedge she called out to him:

"What, without your horse, soldier, and in such a hurry!"

"I am, old woman. The whole world moves towards destruction and we must hurry with it. Today we shall fight a war that will decide all things."

"Pause awhile, soldier," said the old woman in her slow voice. "Tell me what you hope to gain this time from wearing your battledress."

"Life, old woman — my life, your life, all of our lives. We fight this day to go on living."

"A strange fight that," said the old woman.

"Yes," said the soldier, a little wearily. "And I who am not as young as I used to be, must fight whether I like it or no."

"Good cheer," said the old woman. "I shall look for you on the homeward journey."

The soldier marched on in his dull uniform that merged into the brown trees and the dusty road. He joined the ranks of all the other dull uniforms, and held his back straight as a ramrod when the enemy came — from behind, from above, from beneath. There was no time to stop the earth in its helter-skelter progress in all directions. Stone was blasted into atoms, and when the soldier finally emerged a great silence had fallen over the world. All around lay trees, felled to the ground. The only living thing that rose above them was the man himself.

Nor did he meet any living creature as he limped back

through the grim landscape towards his starting point, until he came to the old woman's cottage. There he paused and watched as her old limbs knelt and her gnarled arms slowly dropped a chopper into a pile of wood.

"It is a new task you have there, old woman," he said wearily. "Have you no son to chop this wood for you?"

"My third son," groaned the old woman, "was this day felling trees in the forest. One blow went amiss and now he lies breathless beneath a fallen trunk. I must chop my own wood."

She looked up at the soldier.

"I see you have won again, soldier, you have fought for life and you have come through the battle. You are again the victor."

"I hardly know whether I am or not," said the soldier. "I have met no living creature on my way except yourself. Have you not noticed the strange silence?"

Together they rested and listened. Then the soldier said:

"Your words have proved true. I have lived a long time."

The old woman cackled suddenly.

"When you first rode out to fight, did you not want to be famous throughout the world? See, now, you are become Emperor of the world."

The soldier groaned.

"And you, old hag," he said, "are you to be my Empress?"

The woman nodded.

"I thought when I first saw you," she said, "that you would be a fine man for looking after me in my old age. I have had to wait a long time. But now you may lift the latch and come through the gate. Your rest and your work both await you here. There is grain to be carried from the mill, water from the well, and logs from the wood."

"Are you a witch?" cried the soldier. "Have you cursed me with long life as a trick for your own ends?"

"Nay," said the old woman. "I did not curse you with

65

your wars. You made those yourself. And now you have none with whom to fight, come into my yard. For I have a notion this time to be the victor."

As the soldier lifted the latch and entered the old woman's yard, she laid down her chopper before him and hobbled away to the seat where he had first seen her. There she lay back and composed herself to sleep in the sun.

THE MAGIC POOL

Jonson was a very cowardly fox. His father Renard had been a bold fox and his mother Simca was a brave fox, but poor Jonson had never been anything but timid.

His mother finally got to the point of warning him.

"Remember, Jonson," she would say, "you are not a brave fox. Therefore you must be particularly cunning. Most of us foxes are cunning to begin with but you must be specially bright. That's how you'll make your way. If you're not cunning enough you'll die from lack of food and rot like dead wood. So see to it that your brains aren't wooden to begin with, and you could do all right yet."

So Jonson set out one fine day, determined to prove the most cunning fox in the whole forest.

But dinner-time came and he still had no idea of how to obtain food. There were plenty of woodland creatures around but if he chased them it might mean coming out into the open where there could be danger — other foxes jealous of their prey, or bigger animals, or men with packs of dogs and guns. He'd heard about these things from his family so he preferred to lie quiet or slink quickly through protective undergrowth.

When night-time came he lay down and thought longing-ly of the many tasty rabbits his father used to bring home and the stews his mother used to make. It was just no good, he'd have to find some way of attracting his prey since he daren't go out after it.

He realised suddenly he was beside a pool. He drew him-self slowly towards it and looked down. Oh, what a miser-able frightened face stared back at him. He was startled even by his own reflection. Definitely he would have to do something the next day. He put his head between his paws and thought. Now if he could just get some of the creatures of the forest to drown themselves in the pool he need only wait until their bodies floated to the surface and then he could take a long branch and drag them out. He didn't know much about drowning but it seemed to him a reasonable way of having his dinner ready washed. But what creature in its right mind was going to drown itself in order to feed him? The fox sat down and went on thinking throughout the night.

The next morning he gathered together a large stack of acorns making a great deal of noise as he went, scraped out the insides of the acorns and scooped up water in them from the pool. Then he carefully set down the full acorns in a row where they could be seen very easily. He was aware after a short while of a pair of eyes watching him from the other side of the pool. Then he glanced up and caught a brief glimpse of a young rabbit disappearing from view.

"Good day, Miss," he called.

Then he carried on with his work, singing happily.

Soon he saw the rabbit creep out to the side of the pool. She was a very pretty rabbit with large soft eyes. He smiled and nodded at her but made no attempt to do anything but go on filling his acorns.

"Ahem!"

He paid no attention.

"Ahem!"

"Oh, are you still there?" he asked. "I don't have time to talk, even to a pretty lady like yourself. I'm too busy."

She was caught by his flattery.

"Oh," she said blushing, "do you think I am pretty?"

"Most certainly," he said. "I'm only sorry I don't have time to stop work."

"Why, you're only filling acorns with water," she said.

"Yes, but what water!" he exclaimed. "A magic pool, my dear lady, likely to disappear any time. I'm gathering some of the water to take back to my friends in case it is no longer here when I come again."

"Is that so?" she said. "Maybe I'll take a sip of it."

She drew close to the pool and gazed down. Definitely a very beautiful reflection, she thought, as she admired her glossy ears.

"Yes," she said, "it does taste a little different. But what are the magic qualities it has?"

"Well," said the fox, "I'll tell you. That one sip you took will give you one week more of youth and beauty. The more you drink of a magic pool the longer you'll stay young and pretty."

"Really," said the vain rabbit, thrilled by the prospect of eternal admiration. "Then I must drink again."

"Ah," said the cunning fox, "but it has more magic qualities than that."

"Tell me," begged the young rabbit. "Please Mr. Fox, tell me."

"Well," said the fox, "if you were to put your head into the pool — and you needn't be afraid because you can't drown in a magic pool — you would see. . . something marvellous."

"Oh what?" cried the rabbit eagerly.

"You would see exactly who are your real admirers. Anyone who encounters you at the bottom of the magic pool must love you ever afterwards."

"Oh!" she said. "I'll hold my breath and try it."

So she lay on the bank and dipped her glossy ears and face in the pool, right up to her pretty front teeth. Then a second later she came up, shaking off the water.

"I couldn't see a thing," she declared.

"You didn't go far enough down," said the fox. "It's because you're small. You'll have to dip in a bit further and look straight down and think of how beautiful you are."

So the rabbit tried again, and leaned further into the pool.

"A bit further," cried the fox. "You can't drown, remember. Can you see to the bottom yet? Further —"

"Plop!"

The rabbit's white tail had followed right into the pool. She was heading straight for the bottom.

The fox smiled with delight. It was a shame, but she'd be such a tender morsel. He sat watching the pool.

Soon he became aware of another creature watching the pool and at the same time giving the impression that he was not watching the pool. It was a cat sitting on the far bank. The fox addressed him.

"Good morning sir. I see you also have found the magic pool. Were you thinking of trying it out?"

There was no answer. The cat ignored him completely.

"Of course you know what you would see inside that pool," continued the fox. "I expect the other cats have told you what a marvellous repast there is for whoever puts his head beneath the surface. After all, you can't drown in a magic pool."

The cat looked wise and simply licked a paw. These cats are tricky creatures, thought the fox, and not easily convinced.

"I have heard," he said, "that the menu for you cats is truly excellent. Fish from every part of the world served in the best wines. The pinkest crab, the finest caviar, the freshest salmon, the tenderest turtle, all on silver dishes. And the dishes themselves," finished up the imaginative fox, "will have your own name engraved on them."

He paused for breath. The cat hadn't moved or even looked in his direction.

"All right," said the fox huffily. "I have no more time to talk. I have to get on with my work."

He turned his back and busied himself with his acorns.

There was a splash behind him. He turned to see a furry tail disappearing beneath the surface of the pool. The fox felt quite amazed at his success.

But there was one more visitor yet — a matronly goose who had strayed from a neighbouring farm in search of her young son. The fox smacked his lips when he saw her plump sides.

"Welcome," he called, "to the magic pool."

The goose was ready to run at sight of the fox but she merely heaved her fleshy sides rather than making any great speed. Since the fox seemed to wish her no harm, she relaxed her efforts at escape.

"There are a good many of your neighbours down there," called the fox, "enjoying the health-giving waters of the magic pool. I take it you've come to join them."

"I'm looking for my son," said the plump goose.

"That'll be him," said the fox, "down there. He went with the others. After all, it's not every day one finds a magic pool."

"Not underwater!" cried the horrified goose.

"No one can drown in a magic pool," said the fox. "I expect if you put your head in you'll see him with all those friends of yours. They said to invite you to join them. There's a great party going on down there. They say that the waters have slimming powers."

"Have they really?" said the goose, panting with all her flesh. "Well, I wouldn't mind a bit of company. I'll just have a look."

"Three," counted the fox as the water splashed. "Better get a branch to drag them out."

For a long time he sat on the bank, waiting. Time passed and still nothing happened. The fox became uneasy. Surely they should be appearing on the surface by now. That goose would not be so tasty if she soaked in too much water.

Then an amazing thing happened. A head bobbed up near the far bank — a pretty head with long ears. The young rabbit scrambled out of the pool and shook off the water. Then she caught sight of the fox.

"Oh Mr. Fox," she called, "it was marvellous. You were so right. I have been flirting with all my admirers and I feel as if I shall never be older than I am today. Bless you Mr. Fox."

She blew the astounded fox a kiss before she disappeared into the forest.

Then slowly and with great dignity a long feline shape emerged from the pool. The cat looked neither to right nor left but merely licked his mouth and whiskers. He looked a great deal fatter than before.

As he stalked off, the waters again opened and gave up a spritely and merry-looking goose dragging along her young son. From their chatter the fox gathered there had been quite a party.

But Jonson was in too much of a state to appreciate their merriment. He crept slowly up to the pool. Was it truly a magic pool? Could it really give one's heart's desire? Supposing, just supposing, he were to put his head under the waters. Perhaps he would have the whole run of a farmyard beneath those waters. Perhaps he would change from a timid fox into a bold fox.

Jonson looked at the water and slunk away. He wasn't brave enough to take the risk. Just supposing it didn't work after all and he was drowned! No, he'd better stay safe and cowardly.

A moment later a white-bearded wizard appeared beside the pool.

"Dear me," he said, "I get more absent-minded every day. I didn't notice you'd slipped out until I'd gone a thousand leagues. A more troublesome pool I have yet to meet."

Then he picked up the edges of the pool and folded them. The other sides likewise. When he had reduced it to the size of a handkerchief he popped it in his pocket and disappeared.

The fox gazed in amazement at the flat ground in front

of him. Not a drop of water anywhere, not even in the acorns.

With a great howl of fury and hunger he turned tail and fled through the forest straight back to his mother's lair and his mother's delicious stew.

DRAGONS GALORE

Samuel was a dragon who had lately arrived in the neighbourhood of Ballyditch. He took up residence in the crofter's cottage on the hill overlooking the town, after the poor man had run away on sight of him.

The whole town was in an unholy dread of Samuel. A dragon was such an unknown quantity. One knew how to deal with the grocer who underweighed the vegetables or the goldsmith who overcharged or the bank manager who locked himself away with everybody's money. These were all problems one might run into and one might win or lose over them. But nobody had ever dealt with a dragon before and nobody knew what the result of dealing with a dragon might be.

However, Samuel settled the doubt for them. He established himself first of all as a very bad-tempered dragon. If the townspeople came too near, or if they didn't bring food to the stone stile every day at dusk, or if. . . well, the result might be something terrible. He could breathe smoke, he could set all their houses on fire, he could spread great shiny wings and descend like the monster he was upon their little town. So they obeyed every whim of Samuel's, leaving him feasts of dainties, of newly baked bread and fresh fruits and tender chicken.

Nobody, of course, ever went near the crofter's cottage to have a close-up of this wonderful creature. If they had, they would have seen a very plain animal, not especially large as dragons go, nor especially handsome, nor especially bright in colour. In fact Samuel was a young dragon and a very ordinary one at that.

It was by pure chance that he had come upon the crofter's cottage, and finding it empty had taken it over as his home. He found it very comfortable to lie the full length of the floor and breathe smoke up the chimney. It made a good shelter, with a nice smooth clean floor, and with the chimney there was no danger of his setting the place on fire while he was sleeping.

Then the townsfolk were so obliging. He soon discovered how frightened people were of him and that not only would he be left in peace but he could get them to do everything he wanted — even to providing him with sumptuous feasts.

Samuel had soon learnt the trick of appearing on the hillside at a certain hour of the day when the sun was just right for catching his scales and making them reflect the light, so that to the townspeople he seemed a most magnificent and frightening creature. He would pace up and down breathing fire and smoke and stretching his wings as wide as he could. It was a bit of a strain as Samuel was rather lazy, but it paid him in the end. So twice every day, he breathed fire and stretched.

One day when Samuel was resting after his morning's performance, a knock came on the door. It was such an extraordinary thing that Samuel was too surprised to move for a minute and a half. He was spread out as usual over the nice cool floor. The poor crofter's bits and pieces had been pushed against the wall to allow Samuel extra room to roll from side to side.

At last he drew himself up ready to gnash his teeth and rant fearsomely at whoever had dared to approach this close to the dreaded dragon's lair. Samuel never had a very smooth appearance. In fact the scales on his head never lay orderly as they should, but stood out at tufted angles. Not even scraping his head against the ground could improve on the bad-tempered appearance this gave him. Today, however, he looked more dishevelled than usual, having been disturbed in the pleasant glow of a nap. Today Samuel looked *very* bad-tempered.

He made a rush at the door, determined to scorch the clothes off his visitor with one puff from his nostrils, threw it open, and there on the doorstep sat *another dragon*.

Whatever else Samuel expected it wasn't another dragon, not here at the crofter's cottage overlooking the town of Ballyditch — his town! Moreover, this was a dragon totally alien to Samuel. This was a very smooth dragon. The newcomer showed no surprise at seeing Samuel but addressed him politely.

"Good-day to you, dragon. I thought I was on the right track when I heard something had happened in this neighbourhood. I have been appointed to keep account of all dragons. May I come in and talk to you?"

Samuel's fury had dropped to a mere lashing of his tail. He allowed the stranger to enter, then he went and sat in a corner of the cottage in his straightest and most uncomfortable position.

"I don't know you," he said discouragingly.

"I'm a census-dragon," said the newcomer.

"What's a census-dragon?" asked Samuel.

The stranger coughed and said:

"It's my job to find out how many dragons there are abroad in the world, where they are, and what they are doing where they are, and why it is they are not somewhere else. . ."

Samuel was lost. Now the stranger was pulling out from his folds a long skin parchment and asking him to answer some questions.

Samuel felt important again.

"Name?" asked the dragon smoothly.

"Samuel."

"Age?"

"Two hundred and two," said Samuel without hesitation.

The smooth dragon paused, blinked up at Samuel with

81

one eye and surveyed the scratches he had made on the parchment with the other.

"One hundred and sixty-seven," Samuel corrected himself rather crossly.

The smooth dragon hesitated a moment before deciding to accept this new figure.

"One hundred and sixty-seven," he pronounced slowly, scratching with great care.

"Any family?" he asked next.

"None," said Samuel proudly.

The dragon wrote down "Orphan".

"Where's your home?" he asked.

"Here," said Samuel.

"Nowhere else?" asked the dragon, rather surprised.

"Only here," said Samuel fiercely.

"But before here. . .?" asked the dragon.

"Here and there," said Samuel.

"Who owns this cottage you stay in?" asked the dragon scratching furiously.

"I do," said Samuel puffing himself out.

The dragon coughed.

"You mustn't mind my saying so," he said, "but you're a very young dragon to be living alone without a family and so far from dragon territory. I've travelled for days now and not spotted another dragon in these parts."

"I'm glad to hear it," snapped Samuel. "It means I shan't be having any more visitors. Have you finished, because it's time for my nap."

The smooth dragon tucked the parchment into one of his folds and prepared to leave. Samuel watched him cross the hillside and trundle slowly down towards the next valley.

"Well," said Samuel, "thank goodness he's gone. I only hope none of the silly townspeople saw him or they might. . ."

He wouldn't finished the remark, not even to himself.

What he might have said was — "They won't think I'm so special if I'm not the only dragon in their lives!"

So Samuel settled down again to his nap, though the floor didn't seem quite so cool as it had done before. Or perhaps Samuel was a little more heated than usual. His sleep was shot through with very uncomfortable dreams of a dragon with a smooth head saying:

"Age?"

"Five hundred and one," Samuel heard himself saying.

"Would you say you were a young dragon?"

"Definitely not."

"Have you ever been a young dragon?"

"Never."

"Have you ever been a truthful dragon?"

"Never."

"Family?"

"Never."

When he awoke, Samuel had a vague feeling that he had said something wrong but couldn't quite recall what. Whatever it was, he remained in a state of snappishness for some hours and was very irritable when he puffed and roared out on the hill at sunset.

However, he returned to normal after he had tucked in to a good meal, for the townspeople certainly made tasty pies. Time passed and Samuel recovered from the census-dragon.

Knock, knock! Samuel jumped up with all the scales on his head protruding at irregular angles. Who had dared? Whoever had dared to knock at his door had never seen a dragon's eyes glow red.

He made a rush headlong and flung open the door. He really couldn't believe it. There on the doorstep sat ANOTHER DRAGON. This was not at all like the last. This was a smart cock-a-hoop dragon who walked straight into Samuel's home and said:

"You must be Samuel Dragon — thought I was on the

right trail when I picked up the scent from the old boy doing the census. Nice cool floor you've got here. Mind if I have a stretch on it?"

Before Samuel could say a word the dreadful creature had made himself quite at home in the cottage.

"Who are you?" Samuel gasped in rage.

"Danny Detective Dragon. Private missions undertaken. Goods found. Relatives restored. The lot!"

"You're a New Town dragon," said Samuel in sudden awe.

"Dead on the nail. You're a lot brighter than I expected."

Samuel wasn't really feeling bright. In fact he was gaping at the stranger. The New Town colony of dragons had quite a reputation for slickness back in old Dragonia where Samuel had come from. He'd often tried modelling himself on them. Even his present excursion, his stay in Ballyditch, his terrorising of the townsfolk, was all after the pattern of New Town behaviour. And to think there was the real thing stretching on his own cool floor. But the slick stranger was speaking to him.

"Set on by your old family, you know. Bit desperate about your leaving. Thought you might have slipped in to New Town. Pity you didn't. Easy job finding you there. You'd have stuck out a mile. What got into you, son, to come out this way? Nothing out here you know."

"I'm doing all right," gulped Samuel. "I'm of age to be on my own you know."

"Wouldn't have thought there was much round these parts. Only small fry out here. People not worth bothering with. Why don't you come home with me now? Family all anxious. Precious as gold-dust you are to them. What about it?"

"I don't want to," said Samuel crossly. "I'm important round here and I'm not leaving."

"Well, well," said Danny Detective Dragon, his bright eyes skimming round and taking in every detail of Samuel's little parlour. "I guess even you might make a show out in a backwood like this. Let them know when I get back. Mission accomplished. Nothing more."

With this last remark he was off as pertly as he had entered, leaving Samuel dejected at the thought that it was only a small backwater and not the great big river of life he'd embarked on in Ballyditch. It took him several days of bad-tempered puffing at the townsfolk to work off that discontent. But the luscious pies won in the end. Samuel had a greedy stomach and could be won over, calmed down, and smoothed out by anyone bearing a gift of food.

It looked as if his family had discovered his whereabouts at last. Much good it would do them. He wasn't going back. So dull it was in Dragonia, an adventurous dragon like Samuel, an intelligent dragon like Samuel, a brilliant dragon like Samuel, never got a chance to be himself. Just look how he'd prospered since he'd set out to find his fortune. Even if Ballyditch wasn't an exciting place, as the detective dragon had hinted, still he could move on from there to bigger and better towns. The time wasn't far off when there would be carpets laid out for him and kings tying up their daughters to present to him. He'd have buildings specially built for him with the coolest of cool floors. Oh yes, Ballyditch was only a beginning. He'd move on when it suited him — when the food ran out. Let his family enquire for him then!

What a dreadful noise there was outside. Such blowing and panting and rattling. Whatever could be on the road leading to the dragon's cottage? Samuel braced himself for a show of fire.

Opening the door rather cautiously this time, he peered out. It couldn't be true. It just couldn't be true. It must be his bad eyesight or something. . .doubling the horror that he saw. There before him was a whole troupe of dragons. . . one. . .two. . .three. . .two more.

"Holy dragon-smoke," said Samuel. "It's *them*."

Five members of his family were trundling up the hill

towards him with their well-known rumbling walk, troop-
ing past him into the cottage, covering every square inch of
his nice cool floor.

"Well, well," began his father, an absolutely huge dragon
with a large paunch, "a fine dance your son's led us,
mother , I must say."

"Sammy, whatever is this place you've got here?" put in
his mother. "Why didn't you come and let us know you have
this nice cool floor? You know I like to see these things."

"I was just on my way," lied Samuel. "It took time to
find it and settle in."

"It's too far from home," said his father.

"No, it isn't," said Samuel. "I'm of age to live where I
like. And I like it here."

"Show us round, will you, Sammy," said his mother,
who was a prancing dragon eager for anything new. "What's
it like out there on the hill? What place is that down in the
valley? I'm dying to see it all."

"Not out there," said Samuel quickly. "There are
people out there."

"What's people?" asked a frisky youngster — Samuel's
terrible sister Trudi. "I've never seen people."

"You're not going to see them," said Samuel crossly.
"They're mine. I mean, you have to be careful or they'll
gobble you up."

Trudi was a mistake at all times but now she had begun
to cry.

"Well, Samuel, this is a nice little adventure for a young
dragon," said his uncle in a jolly voice that made Samuel
squirm. "As I always say, young dragons will be young
dragons. You've got to let them feel their way. They come
to develop sense in the end. Have you enjoyed your little
adventure, Samuel? Not getting lonely on your own yet,
are you?"

Samuel puffed hard.

"Come and tell your aunt Matty all about it," said Aunt

Matty with a plump smile. Aunt Matty was a cosy dragon and if there was anything Samuel couldn't stand it was cosy dragons.

"I say," said his father, "that you are too far from home."

"Sammy dear," said his mother, "you are really over-heating yourself. You'll set the place on fire."

"Come and lie down next to me on this cool floor," said Aunt Matty soothingly.

Trudi was bellowing loudly for attention.

"Whatever is the matter with you?" said Samuel crossly. "There's nothing going to hurt you here."

"I'm hungry."

"Well — well — you'll have to wait until sunset," said Samuel in confusion, now that all eyes were turned hopefully on him at this last remark.

"What happens at sunset?" enquired his mother, always the most curious of the family.

"There'll be food then," promised Samuel. "People bring me food to the stone stile," he added proudly. Surely it was an achievement to be proud of.

"What do they do that for?" asked his father.

"Because they're frightened of me."

"Frightened of you," echoed his father in astonishment.

"Frightened of *you*," echoed his mother and uncle and Aunt Matty and the horrible Trudi.

"How dare they be frightened of my son?" said his mother tossing her well-groomed little head. "You're not all that bad-looking."

"You don't understand," said Samuel. "I want them to be frightened of me. They give me food because they're frightened of me. They leave me in peace because they're frightened of me. I have this cottage because they're frightened of me."

"You're not turning into one of those nasty layabout dragons, are you?" asked his father sharply.

"My son isn't a frightening dragon," said his mother.

"You're only a tiddly little youngster," said Aunt Matty, heaving her plump sides with laughter. "How can you frighten anyone?"

"They don't know that. . .well. . .*that*," said Samuel. "I'm the only dragon they've ever seen."

"Well then," said his father, "we must tell them the truth. Mother, I think you'll agree with me, we can't have our son going round the countryside frightening folks who've never harmed him. It's not right. It's not how we've brought him up. It's a disgrace to his family."

"I'm of age," cried Samuel stamping his foot. "I'm one hundred and sixty."

"I don't think so," said his father. "I don't *think* so. Mother, can you remember? I've kept no count myself, but I wouldn't say he was a hundred and sixty yet — not yet."

"Yes I am," said Samuel. "I kept count myself. And I tell you I'm quite old."

"Oh, Sammy," said his mother in a grieved voice. "You'll never tell me I've grown so old that my eldest son is a hundred and sixty. Why, I don't feel that myself. And it's not that I'm vain. There isn't a less vain dragon anywhere in Dragonia. But I don't like to think I'm so old yet."

Samuel couldn't bear it. He rushed out to give an early performance on the hillside. Yet really, it was impossible. How could he parade in his usual fashion when he knew his family was watching him? Everything he did made him feel pompous. As he stretched his wings he felt so ridiculous that he lowered them in a great hurry, cutting short his display.

"Whatever was that for?" asked his father in amazement when Samuel returned.

"You'll see soon enough," said Samuel.

After dusk he crept out to collect the food that the nervous townsfolk had deposited by the stile. He had warned his family not to appear. Quickly he swallowed three or four of his favourite pies before carrying the rest of the food back to the cottage.

His uncle picked up each of the last dozen pies in turn, tasted them, bit again, and finally swallowed the lot. Then he said:

"I didn't like those very much."

"There really wasn't enough for all of us," said his mother licking her pretty little lips.

"It wasn't meant for all of you," said Samuel bitterly. "It was just enough for me."

"Well," said his father, picking up the last crumbs, "as I say, we can't have this living off people. I've always brought my family up to work at getting their own living. Plenty of flocks and herbs and greens round Dragonia for the catching or rooting them up. That's the way to do, get your own food."

"It'll wear off — these young dragon's pranks," said his uncle comfortably.

"I'm surprised," said Samuel bitterly, "that more of the family didn't come to visit."

"More are coming," said his father. "Some cousins are bringing your grandparents first thing in the morning. And there's another batch — your mother's side — coming the day after. They're all curious about this place after the reports we received from that detective chap."

"You can't blame them, Sammy," said his mother. "They're so fond of you."

"And it's such a good chance to see the world," said Aunt Matty. "I always said it was just like home. And it *is*."

"But the people," cried Samuel in alarm, "they mustn't see you; they mustn't see any dragon except me. They won't believe in me any longer when they see the whole family."

"You're not ashamed of us are you, Sammy?" asked his mother. "We've tried to bring you up to be a good dragon.

Not like those nasty roughs who live in the New Town. We don't want you to get a bad name for yourself."

"You're too far from home," said his father. "But if you're being obstinate, then we'll move in with you. Not a bad idea to get to know these people better. We might have a lot in common."

"I'm sure we'll be very happy together," said Aunt Matty cosily.

Samuel flung out of the cottage, then flung back in again. Whatever happened, the townsfolk mustn't get wind of what was going on. It would ruin his reputation.

But the next morning, when he saw the venerable grandfather dragon with the trailing tail and the venerable grandmother with her shaky legs being helped up the hill by a host of cousins, Samuel knew all was up. The people were all out gaping at them. The dragon colony spread itself on the open hill in full view of Samuel's subject city.

There really wasn't any point, Samuel felt, in putting on his morning performance. No one would notice among such an array of dragons as littered that hillside.

Samuel wasn't sure what he'd find when he crept down to the stile to see if any food had been left. He found a group of townsfolk gathered there, gazing up at the goings-on the hill.

"There's one coming towards us," said one of the men.

"Oh, he's only a little one," said another. "He must be a youngster. No need to worry about him. Look at that flashing green one up there with the heavy-looking one like a prize-fighter. They seem to be having a bit of an argument."

Samuel had never felt so mortified in his whole life. To be ignored! To be looked past! He, who had lately terrified the whole town, not even to be recognised! It was obvious the townspeople were intrigued by — nay, even enjoying — the little comedy his heavy-footed relatives were playing out.

It was all up. He might as well go home. Even if there were more meat pies, his share in them would be minute. Samuel felt himself shrinking. If he got much smaller he'd disappear altogether. In fact it was time to disappear altogether. He'd go back to Dragonia and put an end to his shame.

So it was that the marvelling townspeople of Ballyditch saw a wonderful sight. An absolute procession of dragons trundled down the hillside, some of them behaving in the oddest fashion, and all of them making a terrible noise — over to the next valley and on into the distance. It looked as if the crofter's cottage was to be left empty at last. The crofter himself began to pluck up courage to move back into his home.

Then suddenly, whoosh! A huge shape with outspread wings and flames issuing from its nostrils had arrived on the hillside. It was a larger creature than the last and was obviously going to settle into the crofter's cottage itself. The whole town shuddered. The town set to once more to bake tasty meat pies. The town acknowledged that it was a captive city.

Danny Detective Dragon knew a good thing when he saw one, though he might not admit it, and as soon as he'd clapped eyes on Samuel's little hideout he'd known it to be a good thing. What more could a dragon ask than that nice cool floor?

He laughed to himself as he thought of poor Samuel, noosed by his family, going back in high dudgeon to Dragonia. Still, he knew Samuel would console himself by remembering what Danny had told him — that Ballyditch was a mere backwater and nothing for a clever dragon to boast of.

As he stretched out on the nice cool floor and nuzzled the edge of the chimney, Danny gloated over his own slickness. What more could any sensible dragon want than this marvellous town of Ballyditch?

THE DESERT OF THE NIGHT

The Caliph counted one hundred and fifty paces from his couch to the rose and japonica garden. As Defender of the Faithful he ruled a territory that stretched from the Pyrennees to the Indus, from Tartary to the lowest reaches of Arabia. Countless were the servants that counted for the Caliph his camels and his oxen and his vassals and his treasures. Here in Baghdad, in the pleasant scented court, swarthy slaves flickered like shadows from corners and walls to do the Caliph's bidding. And even he knew not how many bearded men were waiting to serve him. For the Caliph counted only his paces from his couch to the rose and japonica garden.

The Caliph was sad. Here, amid the golden mosques and the dancing girls and the prayers that he might live forever, the Caliph rested his cheek upon his hand and grew silent. His wisest advisers understood that the time of melancholy comes to all and did not press the Caliph to say what ailed him. There were enough ministers to sit in judgment on the poor and on the rich, to punish the sinners and to protect the innocent. The Caliph need not trouble himself to see or hear any inhabitant of his vast realm. The whole of his life the Caliph had paced through his pleasant court, counting the steps from his couch to the roses, and his silent servants were no more than shadows to the mighty man.

Now the Grand Vizier, thinking to rouse his master, said to him one day: "The fame of the Princess that dwells in Isfahan grows like the pearl, pure and richly bright."

"Let her be brought hither," said the Caliph.

"My Noble One can command all things," said the Vizier, "but the Princess has a state in life that frees her from all bargaining for a husband. She will marry none but of her own choosing."

The Caliph frowned.

"No one," he said, "has a will beyond the will of the Caliph. Prepare all things for my journey to Isfahan."

Now Isfahan lay four hundred miles distant in Persia, and the land between was nearly all desert. So the Caliph set out with his camels and fifty followers from the pleasant oasis of Baghdad on the slow-flowing Tigris. With the rising sun they travelled and with the full sun they sheltered in tents and with the setting sun they moved once more, until the night ripened to their senses like a luscious fig. Then the camp-fires were lit and fifty bearded faces glowed over the flames.

First, however, the Caliph himself rode down the ranks of his men to count their numbers. This was a task he assigned to no second-in-command, it being a tradition from the time of his great-grandfather whose life had been protected by desert warriors. By his faith he had sworn that he would know the number of his men was complete before he rested a night in the desert. So had his son and grandson done on all excursions into the open sands. So now his great-grandson performed the task that was the personal compliment of the Caliph to his followers. No storm could sweep aside one man, no assassin could pick out one of his riders, but the Caliph would know the count at the end of each day's ride. So Allah would give the final peace of the night. For the desert night is precious to him who rides through the desert sun.

Now the Caliph performed his task as a matter of course, expecting no change in his numbers. With fifty followers had he ridden forth and no adventure had occurred to rob him of one of his men. Forty-seven. . . forty-eight. . .He counted without glancing, aware only of their shapes. Forty-nine. No, he was careless in this count and had added one as he went along. The next number could not be fifty, for there was an extra shape a little ahead. Fifty-one.

The Caliph shrugged and turned back, satisfied that he had lost none of his followers.

The next evening, the Caliph followed the same ritual of counting his men before they prepared a meal for the night. The mighty man did not recall his mistake of the day before, until he reached the end of the ranks of men and beasts. Fifty. Fifty-one. Fifty-two.

Now the desert night is a strange time and a strange place. It bears no resemblance to the desert in the heat of day. It is a place of moon and stars and silent stretches of sky and sand. The work of the planets is strong at such times, charming the soul to travel great distances. The Caliph was not moved to utter a word of his mistake as he would have done had it been day. Instead it flew from his eyes and his thoughts into the vast plain of the heavens.

The third day sandstorms came upon them, blocking their progress. By evening the storms had subsided, but each man had drawn deep within his cloak.

Tonight the Caliph might well fear to find men missing. He counted and the number was fifty-three. Should he count again, he wondered? Yet it was unthinkable, that he, the Caliph, should admit to mistaking his own men.

The faces of the whole company had grown white with the pounding sand, but the Caliph felt he was whiter than the dust, and the thought of the number that would not tally bit hard into his mind as the sand had bit into his flesh.

The next day the Caliph watched the progress of his followers. They skirted the villages and kept always together until evening. The Caliph was satisfied that no stranger had joined them. He rode as usual down the ranks, making sure that his mind did not become confused with tiredness. Fifty. Fifty-one. Fifty-two. Fifty-three. Fifty-four.

The Caliph realised with a chill heart that on the previous

three evenings he had made no mistake. Four days had they travelled and each day had added one man more to the Caliph's train. Yet there was no one, he felt, to whom he could say, "I have four more men with me than when I set out." As he gazed around him all men's faces seemed alike to the Caliph. Why should the men themselves know who were their rightful companions and who were strangers?

The Caliph was a bold man and not given to fear, but as each evening approached a dread came over him. Their wanderings and the storms and supplicating villagers prolonged the journey nineteen days and nineteen nights. At the twentieth dawn the Caliph rode into Isfahan with nine and sixty men in his train.

They were welcomed into the Princess' court with true hospitality. The Caliph's men mingled and were lost amongst the Princess's household. The Caliph gazed around and everywhere saw the same bearded faces, the same slippered feet, the same hidden strength that infested the shadows of his own court. Had he sought out his followers he would not have recognized the faces of his own men.

The Princess came to him in the cool of the garden, amongst the dusky olive groves. As she spoke with the Caliph his delight in her words was as great as his delight in her beauty. But the Princess had wisdom also.

"Tell me," said the Caliph one evening when the sun had passed, "how it is that you, a woman, know so much of the outside world that you can teach the Caliph things he has not seen?"

"Mighty ruler of men," returned the Princess, "I will tell you this secret, though it is no secret to those about me. From my early youth my father allowed me great freedom, to be present in company not usually permitted to women. Now that I rule my own destiny, I welcome many strangers to this city of Isfahan and if their company pleases me I beg them to tell me some story of their adventures or to describe some wonder they have seen. In this way I travel the world and watch great events take place.

"Now I beg you, repay my hospitality by an account of one of your own adventures on the journey here. So may I learn wisdom and be acceptable in my lord's sight."

The Caliph was silent. He knew there was but one thing to tell the Princess. Yet how was he to admit that he had entered her gates with nineteen strangers who, for all he knew, might be cut-throats. So he said that he would think that night and answer the following day.

The next evening the Caliph said:

"Most bewitching of women, your understanding has led me to speak what I have uttered to no other. You asked for an adventure that would add to your vast knowledge. If I described cities and mosques and great monuments, I could compete little with the stories already told to you. Listen, rose of the shining city, and I will tell you what befell on my ride hither. We came through desert, through a land barren of men, and met few travellers and saw the meanest dwellings of villagers. Nothing of note, nothing of greatness did we encounter."

"My lord has a soul," said the Princess. "What did the soul encounter on the way here?"

Then the Caliph knew the Princess was the one to whom he must reveal the secret. So he told her of the nineteen nights in the desert and the men that each evening had added to his train.

"I have brought them into this city," he said. "They are here even in your palace. Yet I cannot look around and say exactly: 'This man is my true follower, and this is not.'"

The Princess listened without interrupting but at the end of his tale she said:

"Truly no other traveller has presented so strange a story. My very soul has involved itself in your fate. Yet why does the Caliph not know the faces of his men? There is not one person in my service whose history I do not know, whose family I am not familiar with, whose past and present I cannot vouch for."

The Caliph wondered even more at the Princess's interest in all things around her.

"I have been foolish," he said, "not to speak out at the very beginning, on the first evening, when the first stranger came. But the desert made all men strange. Now, however, I will call my followers, speak to them and note well their replies. Nineteen out of nine and sixty will reveal themselves as untrue men."

So the Caliph resolved and so the order went forth, that the men who had ridden into the city with the Commander of the Faithful should present themselves for his inspection.

They came, soft-footed, obeising themselves before their master and speaking the language of devotion. As the Caliph looked each in the eyes their brown depths yielded him no secrets. A difference of cheek-bone, of nose, of forehead, spelt nothing to the Caliph. They were servants, each of them, to fulfil the Caliph's commands. They were warriors, each of them, to ride with their master and fight at his will.

The Caliph found that among nine and sixty followers he could not distinguish the fifty true men from the nineteen untrue.

Then the Caliph was afraid.

"I have been a soldier," he cried. "I have braved hardship of sand and storm, of hunger and thirst. I have fought for the faith and would have died fighting had Allah willed. No man therefore can doubt my courage. Yet not to know the heart and purpose of those closest to me fills me with terror."

"My lord," said the Princess, "Allah has sent these men to test your inner strength. In token of your faith yield up to him that which is most precious to you."

The Caliph swore passionately that he would lose forever

that which proved most precious to him if heaven would release him from the fear brought by the nineteen desert strangers.

"What then is most precious in my lord's eyes?" asked the Princess.

The Caliph's glance fell upon a ring he wore on his forefinger. Within a curiously-patterned gold band glowed a ruby the size of a linnet's egg. The Caliph trembled when he remembered his oath and saw this most beloved jewel that had delighted his senses since the time he had become Caliph and even before when he had seen it on his father's hand.

He drew it off and gave it to the Princess.

"Take it," he said. "Let it be traded or melted down and the money be used to feed the poor."

So it was done and the Caliph remained in the Princess's palace and delighted in the Princess's presence, but the fear did not leave him.

Then the Princess said:

"There must be something more precious to the Caliph than his ring. For heaven has not found even that gift sufficient to restore his peace of mind."

Then the Princess called some of the Caliph's servants to her and asked them to name the Caliph's most treasured possession. Now these men were warriors and had followed their master when he went forth to do battle. Each one therefore named the sabre which was the Caliph's most jealous guardian.

The Princess returned to the Caliph and said:

"Ruler of all the faithful, there is yet a possession that you must forswear in the sight of heaven. For truly it is more precious to you than gold or jewels. I speak of the sabre that is a sign of your protective office."

The Caliph flinched, for that sabre was the strength of his Caliphate. Men believed that while it was unbroken so his power throughout the world would never lessen. In the shape of the rising crescent it had been carried before his armies. From Tartary to the Indus it was known as the Caliph's right arm.

At last, however, the Caliph said:

"Peace of mind is more precious than the most glorious tributes of victory. I will yield to Allah the gift he gave me when he set me to rule his people."

So the Caliph's sabre was carried forth and the giant blade was broken to show that his faith rested in the strength of Allah alone.

Then it was that a messenger came to tell the Caliph of an uprising in the north and a wild army bearing down upon Isfahan.

"Send me to them with your message," said the man, "but let me bear your ring to prove I come from the Caliph himself. They will not otherwise believe the Caliph is this distant from Baghdad."

Now the Caliph no longer had a ring to send as a sign of his presence. So he said boldly:

"I will ride to them myself. Let them defy me to my face if they dare."

First, however, he told the Princess to gather her followers and travel by a safer route to Baghdad.

"There you will be welcome as my future bride," he said, "if I do not overtake you before you reach my city."

So the Princess, with many sighs and protests, was prevailed on to journey with her ladies and her guards, out of the fair city of Isfahan to the strong capital of Baghdad.

Meanwhile the Caliph rode out into the northern desert with his nine and sixty followers, until the enemy could be seen springing from the sands. Now the mountain tribes were composed of wild and rash men not easily ruled by one they had never seen. Still, the Caliph's name was so great that they would obey even at a distance.

When, however, they saw the Caliph and his followers, they saw only desert riders like themselves. So they did not believe the messenger who said: "The Caliph himself comes."

"Where is his great sabre?" they said. "The Caliph, we know, rides nowhere without it."

The Caliph found he had no means left him to convince them that the Commander of the Faithful was indeed with them. So his small company clashed with the desert brigands who outnumbered them three times over.

The Caliph's men were well-trained and could deal with fiercer foes than themselves. But the day was not good for them. They had been lazy in their stay at Isfahan. The foe was energetic if not skilful. The Caliph himself was handicapped by having no mighty sabre to wield as an example.

The enemy pressed forward and hacked the Caliph's men until the sand was covered with the fallen. Then the Caliph's life was clearly in danger.

A small band of guardians formed itself round the leader and protected him from the onslaught. Wherever the Caliph turned he found a man to save his life. The enemy retreated and were chased, and at the end of the skirmish the Caliph still stood unharmed – with nineteen followers remaining of all he had brought with him.

They turned then and rode straight through the desert in the direction of Baghdad, the Caliph marvelling at the ways of Allah. Fifty men had he brought forth from his city gates, and fifty of his followers now lay face down in the sand. Yet nineteen silent men accompanied the Caliph on his homeward route and lent him their protection.

When evening came the darkness hid the men's faces until the fires were lit. Then the Caliph rode down the narrow ranks in the gesture of counting his few remaining men. Only eighteen were now with him.

The next evening there were seventeen, and on the following there were sixteen. The Caliph saw no man left behind and no man fall. Yet evening by evening there was one fewer in the ranks.

The day before they reached the walls of Baghdad, one silent warrior remained with the Caliph. Together they crouched over a water spring. In single file they rode, the Caliph not deigning to look back. When evening came he rode on — even into the night. Nothing sounded now behind him and the Caliph knew that to stop would be to pass the night alone over his solitary fire.

When morning came he was within sight of Baghdad walls. He entered the gate with a gaily-decked caravan of merchants. The Caliph was white with sand, sun-drenched, and weary. His clothes were soiled and torn. He bore no baggage and had no ring or sabre to indicate his position. With neither money nor appearance he approached a beggarly state.

When he came to his own palace gates and sought entrance, it surprised only him that he was not admitted.

"I am the Caliph," he said.

The guard shook his head.

"Look at me and know your master."

The man stared at him and said:

"Do you think I know the face of the Caliph? Or am I to believe that the Caliph himself would come to this gate and speak to his servant?"

The Caliph understood too well the truth of the man's remark, for when indeed had he shown his face to any of such low rank? When had any but his closest advisers been in his presence? Without followers, without weapons, without court, without processions, how could he prove he was indeed the man they all awaited, worshipped, and obeyed?

The Caliph found he must watch the comings and goings of his advisers in order to come near one who might recognise him. This was not easy, for the Caliph had set the pattern for all who served him, and even his servants kept away from the people of the streets. Once, when he approached one of his own ministers who had paused an instant before entering the palace gates, he was pushed aside by a guard.

"Behold your Caliph!" he called to his minister.

The man turned at the unexpected words, looked full in the weather-beaten face of the warrior, beheld his grizzled locks, and said:

"Remove this beggar. Let him not be hurt for the man is not in his senses."

The Caliph was sorely tried but he was not alone in his trials for there were more faces round him now than he had known in his whole life. The beggars swarmed in the dust and sat in their patient rows against every wall. The Caliph watched the toothless laugh, the cripples crawl, the blind grope.

Being a strong man himself, the Caliph found work carrying merchants' loads through alleys and across ditches. He bent his back beside the ill-treated donkeys and earned his portion of bread by his labour.

News came daily through the streets that neither sight nor sound of the Commander of the Faithful had been reported at the palace. There were rumours growing every day that he had perished in the desert with all his men. More rumours said that the Caliph's nephew would take up his uncle's office and become ruler from the Pyrennees to the Indus.

Meanwhile the Princess remained in the palace, sad at heart for its missing lord. Daily, however, she sent forth food to the beggars that crowded the gate. Ever watchful, ever listening, she heard their cries and was moved with pity to go herself among them and give the starving people their portion.

One day the Caliph came in their midst, begging alms. No longer did he stand forth and say "I am the Caliph", but knelt with the others and awaited his share.

"She will walk by," he thought. "In my humbleness I shall feel her pass."

There were too many for the Princess to speak to all, but she had the gift of remembering every face so that the beggars were known to her as she to them. When she came to the Caliph he kept his head lowered but she waited until he raised his eyes.

"This is a face I have not seen here before," she murmured.

He looked up at her then, knowing his features were past recognition. The lines on his sun-baked face were those of a labouring man, a bearer of burdens.

The Princess looked long and deeply into his eyes and saw the Caliph she had known in her palace at Isfahan.

"Can it be you?" she murmured softly. "Can it be my gracious lord?"

Then the Caliph's heart was near to bursting and he said:

"I have given all now to Allah, and he has refreshed me seven-fold."

So the Caliph returned to his palace and his position. The cares of his past life were bathed away, but not the memory. He did not return to his melancholy couch or to the rose and japonica garden, but beheld clearly all around him and served, together with the Princess, his many peoples.

I'M NOT AFRAID OF DRAGONS

Clopperty, who was known to all as Clop, was destined to do great deeds. His eleven brothers and sisters believed it. His grandparents, three aunts, four uncles, innumerable cousins, and one great grandfather all believed it. In the midst of them glowed Clop's mother and father like sun and moon, and they, together with two family dogs, four family cats, and several wainscot mice, said that Clop would do great things in life. The whole family lived in a ramshackle house in a quiet country town. Clop as the eldest of the young people was first to go to work and his job was carpentry.

It was a good job because wood was plentiful in the forests around and was used for all the building and decorating in the area. Clop had fine prospects ahead of him and worked as cheerfully at his trade as he had in his home. Poor as his family were, no household was more cheerful, and no one believed more than the spritely great grandfather that Clop would do great deeds in life.

Then one day disaster struck. You could see it coming from a long way away if you were used to noticing these things. The townsfolk, however, were too set in their ways to bother about the warnings. At first they thought it might be a thunderstorm brewing. Then great cloudfalls of feathers burst over the little town, feathers of every description from birds of every size and colour. They wafted in day by day as if driven by marauding goblins. The astonished people gathered them up and took them home to stuff pillows and cushions, and still they were unaware of approaching disaster.

An uncanny darkness grew along with the cold. Then a kind of grittiness fell from the air.

"The chimney-towns are miles off," said the astonished people. "We've heard tell of their dirt, but how could it have blown this distance?"

Then there fell along with the dirt all kinds of small creature that dwells abroad in the air — dead bees and suffocated gnats and shrivelled dragonflies and paralysed mosquitoes. Winged insects bounced everywhere larger than grit and lay all round the astounded folk in a black desert.

Then the wind ripped and roared and suddenly split as the real darkness arrived. The dragon came up from the eastern horizon instead of the sun and his wing-span blotted out all remaining light from the little town.

The buildings of wood creaked and shattered. Splinters swept the streets and fields where already there lay the bird feathers and gritted insects. The townsfolk ran in panic for shelter among rolling logs and falling beams. Clop's family like all other families spilt out of their poor abode.

"My stick," cried Great-grandfather, trembling and tottering. "Clop, save us all and get me my stick."

Clop ran like a whirlwind and rounded up the eleven young brothers and sisters, hoisted the great-grandfather on his shoulders, and led them all to the old stone church. Buildings of stone were the only refuge possible to the demented people, for already houses and their belongings were joining the grit and the feathers and all other dead things in the great darkness.

The dragon was above them now, covering the whole stretch of sky with his wings like a black, unwholesome canopy.

When Clop had got the last of the eleven brothers and sisters safely stowed in the stone church, he heard through the throng the great-grandfather wailing pathetically:

"My stick, Clop. How will I go without my stick?"

Without thinking Clop turned and ran against the

swarming multitudes back to the old home to see if he could find the old man's stick. Suddenly as he ran among the shattered, desolate houses, he came to a stop.

"Why," he thought in amazement, "I'm not at all afraid, though everyone else in this town of destruction is terror-struck. Otherwise I wouldn't be standing here now with that monstrous beast up there waiting to pounce."

Clop looked up into the overhanging night.

"Perhaps I could talk to him," he thought. Then cupping his hands round his mouth, for the noise around was very great, he called:

"Ahoy, bully-botcher! A fine shambles you're making of everything here. I can do better than you, for I can put things together and you can only take them apart."

There was no wind now for the dragon had stopped swishing his great wings and tail. Only an awful silence.

Clop tried again, for the enemy was so overwhelming that his shape could not be seen.

"What kind of creature are you?" he called boldly. "What name are we to know you by?"

The silence grew more intense. Then the dragon spoke.

"I am Serpent-cheater. I am the Worm-of-endless-strength. I am the great and mighty Hisser."

Clop thought quickly to himself: what can cheat a serpent but another serpent? What would a strong worm be that belonged not to the ground but to the air?

The dragon continued.

"My tongue alone can rip down walls and my teeth will crunch them to powder."

"A goodly exercise," said Clop, trying hard to place this creature of darkness. From the way he spoke, Clop imagined that he must be of very antique lineage.

"What do you look like?" he asked.

Again there was silence. Clop wondered if the creature had fathomed his purpose and knew that it would be weakness to describe his appearance. He tried once more.

111

"Why can't we see your magnificence, ancient one?" he asked.

The dragon responded to this.

"You are beneath my body and my wings, and they alone are sufficient to blot out light."

"But how are you shaped," Clop called, "for we can see neither beginning nor end of you? For such a powerful one not to be *known* is a sad thing."

"I had a shape once," said the dragon, "but it was my destiny to grow as men's fear of me grew. As their fears are ill-defined in my presence, so I have stretched lengthways and upwards and along and around."

"Speak your name — once," called Clop, "and then I shall tell you the size of my fear. You will become the size of my fear."

"I am Dragon," called the voice, shrill and greedy.

"Then Dragon," said Clop, "I will tell you that I am one who does not fear your race. I am Dragon-shrinker and Dragon-witherer. You will be no bigger for my belief in you, I can tell you."

There was a tearing noise, more terrible than anything that had gone before, and low on the horizon appeared a rim of light.

"He's growing less," thought Clop as the edge of light broadened. "I can see him now outlined against the distant sky."

The dragon was hissing above as if air were slowly being forced out of his body. The atmosphere was lifting.

From north and south the light poured in fast. The dragon's body was rapidly diminishing. Clop watched and waited, now of all people in the town the only one in sight.

The light grew sharp and clear as it does on the edge of rain clouds after a storm has broken. Clop could see the swaying wings taking shape, then reducing and changing until the creature seemed to be suspended like gossamer in the air. The hissing was dying out and was followed by a final dry choking. Then the dragon who had wings like a bird and underparts like a reptile, fell — straight and sure — among a pile of ruined dwellings. With his fall not an atom of darkness remained in the sky.

Then the people came out of their hiding-places to view their strange enemy and the damage he had done. No doubt once he had been a strong and handsome beast, but Clop was right in thinking that he belonged to antique times. His skin was withered in great folds around him. In his pride it had stretched so far across the horizon that even the markings on it had grown dim. The creature lay now shapeless and sunken among the rubble.

The people had a huge task ahead to clear the broken and shattered town and to build it anew. Clop was eager to lead the way in this and the people praised his courage and made him their hero for a day.

Then the great-grandfather, who had regained his stick, waved it in the air and declared that Clop had been sent to them as a dragon-slayer and it was a shame, so it was, to ignore his great gift. He should be sent out round the country to offer his services to other towns in their need should dragons descend upon them. In this way he would gain great honour both for himself and for his own towns-folk, and the gold he would earn would help to rebuild the town itself.

Clop's mother and father were doubtful about the plan, not wishing to part with so valuable a son. But the great-grandfather had long cherished notions of Clop's destiny and declared it so often and so loudly that eventually the whole town became convinced that Clop must advertise himself to the rest of the world as a dragon-slayer.

Clop too became very brave and very proud at these grand notions concerning him and agreed to set forth and offer his service to the first town that should require aid. So the townsfolk began by equipping Clop for the journey.

Now the first town Clop came to was in distress — but

not from dragons. On arrival Clop presented himself to the Mayor and said:

"I am here to offer my service in return for your generous aid. My own town has been besieged by a dragon and money is needed to restore it. I have come as a dragon-slayer. I might say that I am not afraid of dragons. If you have need of me, employ me. If you are satisfied with my service, pay me well."

Now the Mayor was a clever and rather sly man. He certainly had need of someone's aid, for his town was overrun by rats. Although this young man was offering to help them against dragons, he might be equally strong against rats. Surely a man not afraid of dragons would not be afraid of creatures so much smaller.

But the Mayor did not like the idea of paying generously for anything. So he thought of a plan to secure Clop's aid without payment. He welcomed him to the town and said that the next day they would discuss the matter. For the time being it would not be possible to lodge Clop more comfortably than in a huge barn. This barn was specially designed to be turned into a splendid residence, but as it was — perhaps Clop would make do with it in its present condition.

Clop was a simple soul, not used to much comfort, and accepted the barn thankfully enough. What he could not know was that here was the centre of the rat colony and that the Mayor hoped that during the night Clop, coming face to face with the rats, would effect their destruction in the same way that he had destroyed a dragon. The town could then refuse to pay him on the grounds that they had no agreement he should destroy their rats.

So the unwitting Clop settled down peacefully for the night in the barn. The straw was fresh and warm and he was very tired after his journey. Tomorrow would do for thinking about dragons.

After midnight Clop was wakened by the footing of

rats. The barn was lit by a thousand glittering eyes. From rafters and chains and ledges they hung, from floor and ceiling and wall they crawled. They gloated over the sleeping Clop. They scrabbled and rattled and padded and gnawed around and towards him.

With a leap Clop was on his feet and running, terror-shaken, to the door. His path was not direct for he tripped and stumbled over the treacherous brood. The noise was suddenly outrageous. Everything that could squeak or shuffle or rattle or clang, was declaring itself. Clop found the door and fled out into the night with the fanged creatures at his heels. Straight through the town he ran and the rats scattered with him. Into every house they poured and out came the shrieking townsfolk. By morning the rats had more than overrun the town. They were well nigh in command.

The Mayor wrang his hands in horror. At least they had confined the largest rat colony to the barn — up to the time of Clop's arrival. Now he had done the worst thing possible and set rats free to ravage every dwelling. Who would have thought that it was possible to be afraid of rats and not afraid of dragons!

"They're not the same thing at all," cried Clop. "I told you it was dragons I was prepared to deal with. I am not afraid of dragons, but I *am* afraid of rats."

"Go," said the Mayor in fury. "You have done the worst damage possible, young man. Take yourself off to the ruin of other towns than this. We've no dragons here for you and can pay nothing for your services."

Greatly crestfallen, Clop departed and journeyed a long way. Day after day he trudged on, until all signs began to show that he was approaching the chief city of the country. Here dwelt the King, Clop knew, glorious in his palace. Here dwelt all that was noble and wise and wealthy. To this centre all men on the road were hurrying.

It was festival time. The streets were gaily decked and

thronging. Men dressed as beasts and beasts forced to totter like men were the prime attraction. Fools in rags and beggars in sumptuous robes assailed all newcomers. Clop was bewildered.

"Men become masters and masters become men on such a day," a fellow traveller said. "Take my advice and play the fool. Then you will be treated as a wise man."

Clop was a simple soul and unused to such follies that the city offered. When he was hailed by those around to say what he did there, he answered truthfully:

"I am a dragon-slayer. I have come from my country town to offer my services in your need, should dragons assail you."

Nothing could have appealed more to the wits around.

"To court with him," they called. "Bring forth some dragons and let us see him slay them."

Laughing and joking they hustled the astonished Clop before them. The cry was taken up by others, and suddenly Clop was the centre of entertainment. Long before they reached the court cardboard weapons had been handed him, follies and fripperies draped him, and the people called loudly for "Dragons".

Just outside the palace, men dressed up to look like fearsome monsters appeared.

"Kill the dragon for us," hooted the populace.

Clop found himself in a throng of hobby-horse monstrosities, each charging at him and nuzzling him and encouraging him to lash out at them. He floundered, horrified, and the people cheered.

They were carried onward into the courtyard of the palace where the chief entertainment was going forward. Before the King and his court Clop was forced to perform his foolish prancings and stabbings. Nowhere could he escape from being the hero of the day.

"Well done, Dragon-slayer," called the King.

"Sir," called Clop, "help me."

"What does the dragon-slayer say?" asked the King, astonished.

"I am a dragon-slayer," called Clop. "A real dragon-slayer."

"Why, the poor boy's wits are gone," said the King. "Let him come close and I'll speak with him. He has been teased enough by this make-believe foolishness."

So Clop reached the King and told him truthfully what he had entered the city to do, that dragons were real and that he was not afraid of them. Now the King was wise in the ways of the world and could see that Clop was neither a fool nor a liar. But the King was not wise beyond the ways of the world and he did not believe Clop's story of the dragon.

"Your journey here is useless, young man," he said. "We have never known dragons in this city. We men fight each other here and leave people in country towns to think about dragons. Go home and continue with your carpentry. These notions of yours will disappear in time."

Now Clop had not travelled so far without learning some wisdom also, and he saw that the King was right — that he had no place in this chief city whose men were so wise they could safely act the part of fools. So he promised the King that he would return home.

"I like you, young man," said the King kindly. "You take your dragons too seriously, but still I like you. Take home with you some of my gold and let it be used for re-building your town. You can say quite truthfully you have earned it fighting dragons, for there are all my jesters weary with baiting you. You have outbreathed them all."

"Since the gold will help my town," said Clop, "I will take it. But let it not be said that I have killed your dragons, for here no man fears them. When your dragon comes only one who knows fear will be able to serve you."

The King's eyes sharpened at Clop's words, but the youth had gone, leaping from the King's dais and out through the courtyard. He returned home with the gold.

His own town welcomed him, for in truth they had lost a good workman when they sent Clop journeying into the world. The gold was valuable but even more so was Clop's skill in carpentry. Even the great-grandfather was pleased that Clop had come home.

The rest of the world might not believe that dragons existed but Clop's own townsfolk knew better, and among them he remained a hero. For his great-grandfather he carved a beautiful dragon-headed stick of which the old man was very proud.

THE ADVENTUROUS SEAGULL

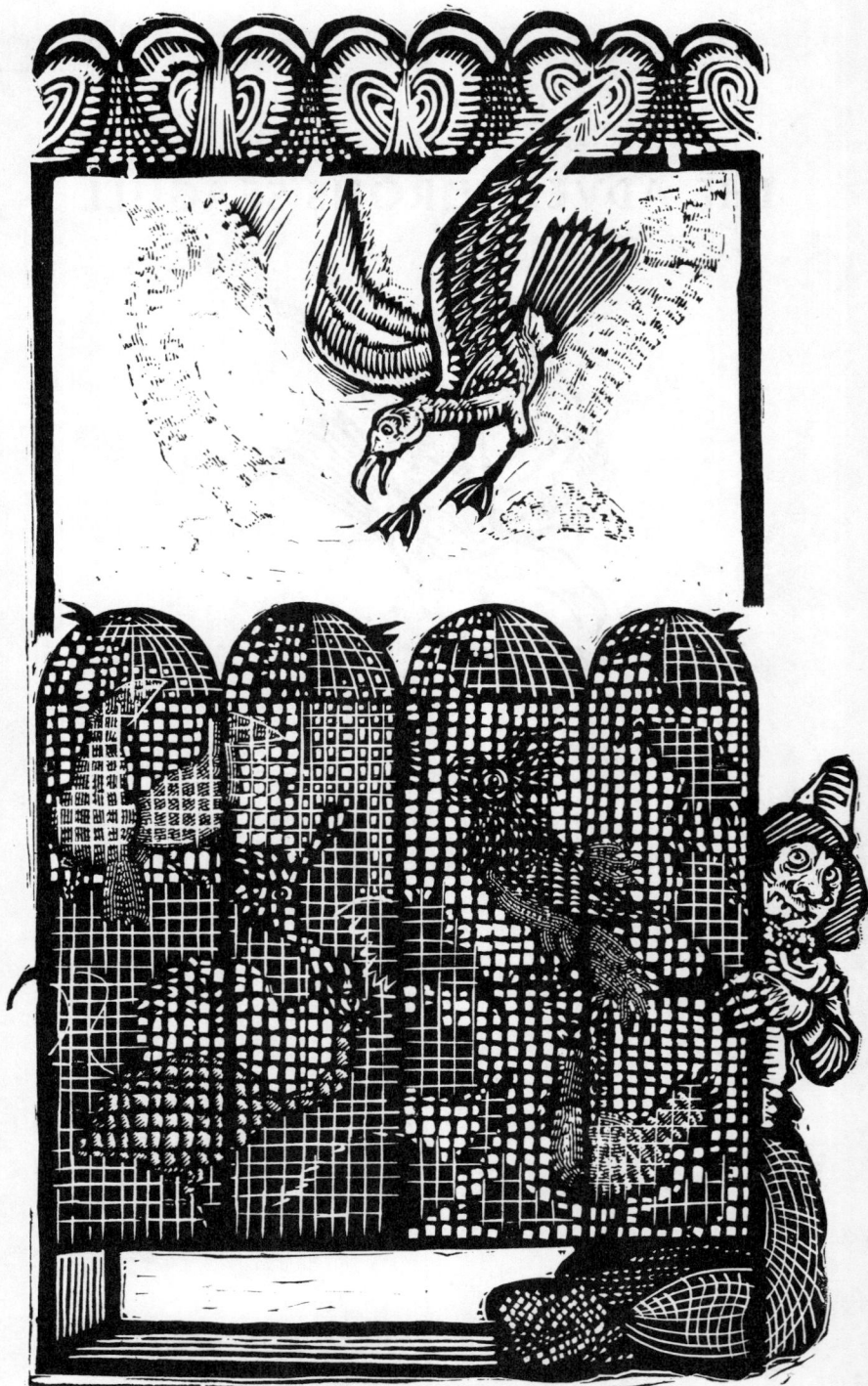

Swinging. The sea was swinging as it had always done. The curlews were crying as they had always done. The wind was strong on the gull's breast and the spray was bitter in his eyes.

All the sounds of the sea sang to him as they had always done, and the louder they sang the more restless he became. The migratory birds were going now. The petrels were passing the rocks with strange tales. Gannets were winging south. The gull's heart was fired with rage and envy. Only his clan, it seemed, inhabited the same shores, sleeping and feeding with the same tides.

Today, he knew, would not come again. Today he would tell his father his intention.

"May I ask — ask — ask —" he piped from his clear young throat.

The gulls descended, surrounding his father with a deal of flapping.

"It is time," cried the young gull, "to fly afield. I shall go from these rocks."

The others screeched aloud.

"To leave —" "to travel —" "to fly alone!"

Suddenly there was a shrill call from the gull's father.

"Foolish bird!"

On vibrating wings the great gull rose, carrying with him the whole company. Finding himself deserted, the young gull preened his feathers, burying his head in warm plumage. Then looking up he saw that he was not entirely alone. There was one bird that had been too old to move.

"Oldest and wisest," he called to the lifeless bundle of feathers, "do you think I am right to go and explore the world?"

121

The little eyes blinked slowly.

"Gull," came the thin voice, "I once had a brother who longed for the excitement of distant shores. He went with the migratory birds one season when they departed."

"Was he killed at sea?" asked the young gull, expecting a tale of disaster.

"The following spring," said the oldest and wisest, "he returned in a state of strange excitement. It wasn't long, however, before he grew dull among us and was as restless as before."

"Ah," said the gull, "I have his spirit and am proud to venture."

His wings hovered lightly.

"I shall return with the spring —"

He rose in the air.

"— with tales you will envy —"

He soared in the soft breeze. A breaking foam of sea and rocks and gulls lay beneath. The birds jerked their heads upward to watch their foolish comrade as he flew out from his own creek and on down the coast.

Ahead came smooth shores and open sea. The gull felt stronger winds and new currents. They drove him inland among human dwellings. He passed coastal towns where he found other gulls feeding on clotted refuse, fat dull scavengers. There he learnt to beg his crusts. Then he continued further inland, keeping at first to rivers but venturing ever onwards into a dryer land.

It was when he was hungry and weary one day that he approached a house that stood alone. A woman came out into the garden and scattered crusts for him.

"Come on, my beauty," she called. "What a glorious flyer you are. No one could put you in a cage."

The gull swooped and seized a crust.

"Where d'you come from, stranger? This is a dry and dusty land for the likes of you."

The gull was scornful of the woman, but being hopeful

of more food he remained hovering above. The woman shook her head and went indoors. The gull swooped and circled and dived at last towards the windowsill.

Facing him in the open window was one of the smallest and most beautiful birds he had ever seen, a bird with feathers of gold. The gull's arrival made it flutter up in alarm but it was forced by the bars of its cage to flutter down again. When the gull realised that this pretty bird was caged he cried:

"Come out and try your wings with me."

The bird twittered excitely.

"I cannot leave my home. The door is locked."

"Must you always be a prisoner?" asked the gull pityingly.

"Sometimes," said the bird cautiously, "my mistress opens the cage door and I have freedom to fly within the house."

"Do you not envy me?" asked the gull.

Now the bird grew annoyed at the gull's boasting.

"No. I am a delicate creature, not able to exist out in the open. I have too many enemies. Here I am protected and given food. Not for the world would I be a beggar like yourself, gull."

"I pity you," said the gull proudly. "You have no spirit."

"Not for a life like yours," snapped the little bird.

The gull went on his way, disappointed. He was now driven by winds that carried no scent of the sea. He flew alone and hungry for countless miles until one day he arrived at a town square full of traders. The strangest thing of all in the midst of the dust and heat and noise was a huge cage filling the centre of the square. It was filled to overflowing with birds of every description, from all lands and of all colours, for here was the largest bird market in the world. Thousands were sold daily for rich men's tables, and thousands were sold daily to fill smaller cages, but not one was sold for freedom.

The gull soared high above the ribs of the cage, amazed at the sight. The caged birds drooped sadly until suddenly they noticed the gull.

"He is free," they called in amazement. "Speak to us, stranger, tell us what it is like to be free."

In spite of his weariness the gull spoke to them then. With long piercing cries he recalled the freedom of rocks and pools and foaming waves. Here at the peak of his travels he spoke to the imprisoned birds of his home.

The noise led to his undoing: one man in the throng beneath caught the sound and looked up. Could there be profit in a seabird so many miles from the sea? The hungry gull paused in his tale and glanced greedily down. There on the ground lay something white. He dived quickly but had hardly alighted when he felt the fall of the net around him. It was a private trader who had trapped the gull and who clapped him into a tiny cage of his own where his sides were so cramped that he could not raise his wings. Lean and weary, the gull was put up for sale while the birds in the common cage called mockingly to him:

"Sing us a song of freedom now, gull."

Although seabirds were rare in this part of the hot and dusty world, the gull was not bought quickly for he had been reduced by his travels to a mere shadow of his former self. One day, however, there passed by a retired sea captain whom poverty had forced to seek a scanty living inland. The old man's eyes had distant horizons in them and such were his dreams that as soon as he saw the gull the captain knew that here was a true companion. For all the days of his life left to him the gull's cries would remind him of the sea. While he stood there in his shabby clothes the old man felt the rising of strong tides; his beard quivered.

"How much?" he asked.

It was too much to pay for a bird when his purse was so thin. Yet the captain counted out the coins with slow pauses. The cage was pressed into his hand.

So our gull went home with the captain, to a room filled with old pieces of sail and spar and shell. The man ate his scanty meals in front of the bird and fed him alternate bites. Yet in spite of his kindness the gull pined miserably in his cage. At times he gave vent to his imprisoned heart, and the captain heard in the gull's cries the changing tides, great storms and mighty calms. The gull sang of his joy when he first rose in the air and took his own way. He remembered the breeze on his wings, now beaten down as he strove to raise them by the cruel bars. Then the cage brought to mind the imprisoned birds in the market square. All the hunger and discontent he had known on his journey lived again in his pitiful cries.

The captain called to him to stop.

"Tell me," he said, "of how the ships rise on great waters."

But the gull sang only of his misery until the old man could bear it no longer.

"It seems, my friend," he said, "that there is one answer for both of us. We are many miles from the sea here, yet let us try once more to reach our home before the end of our days."

So saying, the old man gathered up his few possessions, took his pack on his shoulder and the gull's cage in his hand, and set out on his last journey back to the sea.

The captain's small store of money did not carry them far. When it was gone he travelled on foot, selling his possessions piece by piece to pay for food. After that, they begged their way. Slowly they crossed the great land mass. For many weeks they met no man who had seen the sea. For many more weeks the gull was carried step by step back to his home country.

They were still several miles from the coast when the gull recognised the tang in the air. Raising his bedraggled head he uttered his first cry in many days. It rent the old man's heart with joy and he hurried forward as fast as his legs would carry them. As they drew nearer the sea the gull's calls increased. When at last they came to the stretch of glinting water that meant so much to both of them, the old man set down the gull's cage and said:

"We are home again, the Lord be praised."

Then a thought struck the captain. He looked down at the cage and realised that one task still remained. His gnarled fingers groped at the catch. He had no sooner lifted out his companion, however, than the gull jerked free, mounted high above the captain's head, wheeled giddily in the clear air.

"Come back, gull," called the captain, feeling the loss of his comrade. "We two are seabirds together. Let us keep one another company."

Yet not for an instant did the gull pause now that he had escaped his prison. His bond with the old man was forgotten, the captain's voice grew distant, and only the waves and coast lay ahead. With long curdling shouts the gull took his path homeward. He was dizzy when he arrived at his old familiar creek.

He alighted and paused where a line of gulls stood on the damp beach, their faces turned to the sun. He stood for a while in row with them. Then with hovering leaps he spun towards his father, his brothers, his family and friends. They spread wing when they saw him, swooping and circling in greeting to their adventurous comrade.

For a long time the gull held his audience. Until well into the clear glow of sunset he recited his adventures. Gradually, however, the gulls grew tired of his boasting and began to leave.

"If only," called the gull after them, "you could see the wonderful colours of the birds I saw or —"

But the other gulls had dropped away one by one, leaving the wanderer strangely restless. Was this to be his homecoming?

"Back at the beginning, gull?" enquired the oldest and wisest who had been too stiff to move. Then he added: "Gull, I am too old to envy you, but the other birds are jealous because they have not travelled the distances you have travelled or faced the hardships you have faced. Now they want you to forget what they have never known."

"Alas," said the gull, "that they should never know what it is like to be released from a prison."

His thoughts returned to the sea captain whom he had deserted after all his kindness. *He* understood what the gulls did not. Now he could hear the old man's voice raised by the tide:

"Come back, gull. Let us be seabirds together."

Sharply and steeply the gull rose with a wail that shook his entire body. He could not rest here among his own kind. As the other birds gazed once more after him into the deep sky, the gull set out on the journey back.

THE STORY OF THE OAK

The old oak tree had been there for countless generations — certainly as long as Petro could remember, and even as long as Petro's father and grandfather could remember.

It was a large forest, and because the oak tree was the oldest of all the trees it had the greatest share of memories. Many were the people who had met and parted beneath its boughs; many names and markings were carved into its trunk.

The oak tree, although so powerful and proud that all the trees of the forest looked on it with awe and respect, had not only an old heart but a kindly one. It always took an interest in those who came to laugh or cry into its leaves. Petro was a particular favourite for from his early childhood he had whispered his secrets among the tree's rustling leaves.

The peaceful days, however, were to end, for the land was struck with great misery. For many weeks there was no rain; the crops died and the earth cracked open its parched lips. Men scrambled and scratched for food; animals died from the drought.

Then the forest was invaded by people searching for wild roots and berries that had lain untouched for generations. In the coolness of the oak's wide canopy little processions would take up their stand and pray for rain. No longer did children skim through its boughs with laughter. The oak saw that their eyes now were great balls of hunger. Even the trees of the forest began to let their branches droop and their leaves wither.

The oak, however, was not so quickly affected. His strength would ebb as slowly as it had grown, and he could endure much.

"Little master," he said to Petro one day, "it grieves me to see the sad faces of these people."

"Alas," said Petro, "while this drought lasts we are starving. We have taken from the land all it can offer. There are no more crops and no more water. How can we welcome our empty bellies and dry mouths?"

The oak grieved through every branch.

"You have not taken everything from the ground," he said. "If you cut off my branches, dig up my roots, you will find sap in my old body. Let me quench your thirst in that way."

"Old oak," said Petro greatly moved, "you are most good. Would you offer your life to restore me for just a few hours?"

"Willingly," said the oak. "For you have spoken to me many a time when others have come and gone without a word, thinking I could not understand them."

"My gratitude is too great," said Petro. "I am no beast to feed in this way on a friend. Besides, old oak, although you offer me the sap of your body it will not quench the thirst of all this land."

"What can help you then?" asked the oak.

"I fear that now only God can help us," said Petro. "But although all creatures with souls pray day and night, He gives no sign of having heard us."

"Alas," said the oak sadly, "I have no soul, and do not know how to pray. He would not be likely to hear me in any case if he does not hear you men who do have souls."

"Then, old oak," said Petro, "there is nothing you can do to help us, except go on shading us while life remains in you. And in us," he added softly.

But the oak became more and more grieved at the pitiful sights he saw around him. As time went on he felt the contraction of his own limbs and the dry agony begin to spread within as he had viewed it without.

"What can I do?" he said to himself. "Why can I not for

once be blessed like men with a soul, so that I too can pray. If I could have one I would not demand it forever, just for one moment that I might make myself heard by this God Petro says can put all right."

The other trees of the forest had become very silent now in their agony, and the stillness of the air made the oak restless without allowing him the power to move.

"Do you not long to have souls?" he asked the others, "so that you could join with these people in their prayers. Truly until this day I have been pleased enough to be a soulless creature, for my life has been longer than most and I have had a good share of it. But now when I see all people humbled by hunger I am sorry I cannot implore on their behalf this person they all kneel to."

"Wisht," said the other trees, "and let us sleep ourselves away. Do not disturb the ache within us."

"Do not disturb us," groaned the whole forest.

Day by day the old oak watched for the thin bodies and pinched faces that sought his shade in the glare of the sun. Day by day he missed familiar friends. Still the longed-for rain did not come.

Then one night when everyone and everything appeared to be asleep or drugged with weariness, the oak whose branches were high in the forest noticed a slight movement in the heavens, a darkening of the moon.

"Maybe," he said, "it is this person they call God coming at last to visit them and to find out what they want. But now they are sleeping and they will miss him."

He moaned to himself.

"I must do something. I must let him know, or keep him until daylight. If only I had a soul that he might hear me. Still, am I not amongst the largest in the forest? I will reach up to him with my boughs. Perhaps he will see me, dumb as I am, and pause."

A sudden gust of wind shook his branches into relaxing the tight attitude they had assumed during the stillness of previous weeks. More clouds swept across the moon as the old oak, regardless of the pain within his drained body, raised his branches aloft, letting the topmost spires float on the night breeze. A sound of movement was sweeping through the whole forest.

"I must go higher yet," he gasped. "I must grow taller in my old age. He must see me beckoning him when he approaches."

The oak heaved himself up, feeling his straining roots almost crack. The wind tore now at his waving arms, flinging them higher and higher. . .and higher. . .

"Please," cried the oak, "though I have the body of a soulless creature, grant me a soul to be heard at this time."

With the first few drops that the oak felt on his trembling leaves came the swift, bright thrust of lightning, splitting and tearing his body down to the bole, shattering the clouds into a downpour of life-giving rain, and waking the whole world into a prayer of praise and thanksgiving.

When Petro walked through the forest the next day, he found the oak's shattered remains and wept grievously for his old friend.

"Why must it have been you, kind old tree, who was struck down in this way, you who have always shaded us with your arms and protected us with your body. Even now at the end you took the final stroke upon yourself and allowed us to be spared."

So mourned the oak's best friend. Even he did not know the old tree's final triumph.

THE SINGING STARS

Glim, the monkey, pressed his ear to the ground and listened. It was some time since he'd first heard the noise, rising and sinking with the time of day or the heat or the wind. It seemed to him to be getting more frequent. At noonday it subsided slightly.

It was a sound that tempted him to listen; a sound sweet enough to make him stop whatever he was doing and strain to catch the message.

Marga, his wife, had taken their son Uhu up into the trees. It was feeding time. Feeding time happened often. With Uhu it happened nearly all the time. Squealing and swinging with his mother he sang his own monkey prattle. But Glim still caught that other sound, at the strangest times and in the strangest places, over and above Uhu's squeals. Today he felt it in the earth as he pressed his ear to the musky soil.

Marga was quiet while she was with Uhu, but from time to time she swung downwards to discover why her husband lay so long silent. Then she scolded him until he went with her.

Marga heard nothing of the noises Glim listened to. She felt none of their pull and understood none of their power over him. She felt only the call of her young and her motherhood wrapped itself round Uhu like a cocoon.

Glim forgot the noises and went with her, swinging more easily on his long arms, and taking Uhu into the folds of his chest he sat with him, his own possession, in the forest's drowsy time. The foliage covered them as Glim covered Uhu, and Marga stretched backwards along the thick branches, quiet now her husband was at hand.

There was a sudden scent in the air that made Glim

137

creep forward and look down. Marga sniffed too but did not stir. They were safe at that height and she knew that Glim would not venture into danger with Uhu in his keeping.

Glim scrabbled among the leaves, then he swung slowly forward until a space between the trees allowed him to catch sight of a spotted-gold shape. The she-cheetah was beautiful and stealthy as she moved round the trunk. Glim recognised her and he knew that she had come because she too was picking up the sounds. She was alive to them in a way Marga was not, for she had lost her cubs a season before.

Yet even as he glimpsed her below, her back slipped out of sight. Cheetahs are shy creatures. Glim could go no closer because of Uhu, but even so he would not have caught up with her.

All that day Glim thought about the strains he'd heard. Not loud, certainly, but haunting. Not dangerous as the forest understood danger, but joining old longings and new longings together in his monkey breast.

When dawn came, after the feeding time, Marga gave herself wholly to Uhu, forgetting Glim with the renewed joy of tending her young. Her husband swung free and fierce through the upper lanes of foliage. The branches did their job of scratching and slapping his hairy frame.

As he moved towards the marshland he became aware again of the strange piping noise, more like a fragrance than a sound. He would hardly venture further, for over there among the lakes were the settlements of men. Marga would scream if she picked up those scents on him. So Glim went downwards instead, scraping the damp forest floor and catching the sound more fully every second. He must be close upon it now.

Then something shone through the thicket with a brightness that dazzled Glim. He put a forearm in front of his eyes and peered through the hairs. Partly sunk in the ground was a small piece of fissured rock, a slab of star-like formation, that gave off an aura of white light. From this came the strains that Glim had heard during past days, only fuller now, sweeter, more binding. Glim stood, he knew not how long, in a strange ecstasy.

Then as if it had gone through some cooling process the object paled, the noise sank, the light went. Glim dropped his aching arm and gazed astonished at the rough slab in front of him, grey, cold, and soundless.

After a while he approached it. It had a crinkly surface but nothing strange — no light, no living quality — remained to suggest the wonder he had just witnessed. Cautiously he touched it, smelt it, took it in his forepaws and unbedded it slightly from its position in the ground. Just a piece of rock.

He would have carried it off with him but another presence made itself felt. Quicker than the wind the monkey was off treeward, screeching excitedly to the heavens.

The python that approached was a huge creature, lazy though, and sufficiently despising the monkey brood for their lack of subtlety as to take no notice of Glim's disturbance.

Presently Glim swung back when he felt he had secured his position and peeped down at the shining black-spotted coils that rose now in stages as the python settled himself for sleep. He had ringed himself round the slab of stone in total ignorance of its secret.

Glim watched for a while, rubbing the soles of his feet in irritated silence. The python intended nothing more, however, than to sleep, and Glim in time moved homeward. The sounds that had claimed his attention for days past were ended and the forest seemed dull.

Marga noticed nothing except her husband's sulks. These she repaid with scolds and twitches. Uhu whimpered. Glim prowled the branches restlessly.

The next day he went back to where he had seen the

stone and where the python seemed to have found an
abode that suited him, for there he still was. For two days
running Glim returned and looked down from the
branches at the same strong coils.

Then something happened. Glim jumped in alarm as the
python moved more rapidly than you would imagine the
long beast could and his body roped the trunk of a tree
like a coiling spring. There behind him on the ground lay
the object that had the power to shake those thick folds.
Again the stone glowed as Glim had seen it before. Again it
sang — for the noise was like music bursting from the
stone's crevices. Glim listened entranced, and the python
listened, and the whole forest round seemed to listen.

Glim had forgotten what time of day it was until the
sound died away and the stone returned to an ordinary
grey appearance. Then, the monkey moved. Two — three
— four great swings from the tree and he was crouching beside it, heaving it out of the earth and running clumsily
with it pressed to his breast.

Sounds exploded around him as if all kinds of forest
creature had been drawn there and were suddenly aghast
at the monkey — that mad, bad, comical animal — stealing
their singing stone. But Glim didn't care. He was away
with it, through the trees, over the heads of the other
animals, out of their reach, and making for he knew not
where. Certainly not home to Marga and Uhu.

His instinct was to hide the stone, somewhere that only
he would know about. He found a spot between the out-
growing roots of a tree where he could dig the stone down
under the mesh of knotty bark and cover it with soft dank
soil. He had come further round into the marsh areas than
he was aware of.

Then he turned, swaying cautiously from side to side.
Convinced finally that the stone was his own secret, he
went home to his family.

Day after day Glim returned to the hiding-place,

sometimes scraping the soil to peep at his treasure. His
habits were stealthy now and he never approached the tree
without assuring himself that no other animal was near.
The birds he could not control. He watched jealously as
they spiralled above. The stone, however, remained untouched and mute.

Then one day it happened. Glim was resting among
the leaves with Marga and Uhu. They had eaten a meal and
slumber was near. Softly, like the rustling of the leaves
around, came the first strains. Sweetly, like that first sleep
he was drifting into, it touched Glim's senses. Soothingly it
lifted him out of his monkey state until he felt himself
borne like a thing of pure joy above the earth.

Uhu snored gently and Marga was swaying with the
branches, but Glim was awake and alive and loping from
branch to branch, drawn by the sound. This time he knew
exactly where to find its source. It flooded towards him as
he approached the marshland.

But Glim was not the first to appear in that area. A
leopard's spots shone quite distinctly through the trees.
Various chattering bushy tree animals were around. The
ground breathed with burrowing creatures. Glim knew that
other monkeys were not far off. The music drew them like
an enchantment. He could not — would not — approach
the hiding-place with all these around him.

Now Glim discovered that the treasure he had imagined
his own was so wonderful that it could never stay a secret,
never be a peaceful possession. The sounds held their
power over him and all beings that could hear. Far over, on
the other side, there were new noises that made them all
pause in their tracks. Glim recognised suddenly the men of
the marsh country, who built their homes on stilts at the
edge of the great water.

He was more intrigued than most by the appearance of
men. They were a puzzle that stretched his brain to its
limits. Something fearful, something strong, something like

141

himself, yet not doing the things he did, like swinging among trees or scratching their stomachs or going on all fours. They were smooth-skinned too, like the python, except for a crowning crest.

They all stood, however, fixed in harmony until the music came to an end, the rock cooled, and the light that was issuing from round the tree's roots died away. Then the men came forward and the animals moved back. The men were no bigger, no stronger, than some of the creatures around. But they carried weapons, and the area was more human territory than it was forest. So it was the men who reached Glim's tree and who dug around the roots and unearthed the stone. Then they covered it with a cloth and carried it away.

Glim followed them, creeping and leaping and going above and around. When they reached the end of the tree-line he stopped. He watched the men joined by others, by their womenfolk and a swarm of children. He watched them unwrap the stone and show it. He heard noises and saw their teeth shine one to another. Then they took the stone inside one of the houses by the great water.

Glim came and went several times in the days following. He roamed from tree to tree, not daring to venture too far forward. He watched the movements of the men but saw nothing of the stone.

One day, however, it did appear. Some of the women had decided that there was nothing more remarkable about this piece of rock than its attractive shape. So it was given to the children to carry outside and use in their games.

Glim saw it passed among them. He saw it abandoned on the open ground. He watched even at noonday when the people slept. Then when the men had gone forth to their work and the women were indoors, he saw one small child toddle out from his home towards the starry shape lying in the open.

Now the stone began to glow and even to burn, with a

pure cold light. Glim was hardly prepared for the rapture of the stone's song as it lay exposed for once beneath a clear sky. He would not eat again; he would not sleep again; he would exist only at the music's bidding.

From out of the surrounding forest came all kinds of creatures. Glim saw the she-cheetah walk in front of the child. The small one was standing closer to the stone than any other. Fierce creatures swung in and out of its line of vision, all drawn and all held in place by the stone's enchantment. A man limped out of one of the huts at a distance. He had been left behind by the others on account of his lameness. Now for the duration of the music all creatures waited in astonished stillness.

As the stone cooled and the song died, the horror of the child's danger overcame the man. He called, he whooped, he picked up pebbles and took aim at the cheetah. Not just the child wanted to be near the precious rock. There were many animals ready now to approach it.

Women came running from the huts at the noise. They brought rough weapons, brooms and sticks and spikes. The animals retreated, but more slowly this time, loth to leave behind the stone.

The child was snatched to safety, but the man lifted the stone in a peculiar fury and with the utmost force he threw it far out over the great water, until it splashed at such distance from the shore that no creature would be likely to reach it. Then the man's fury turned to weeping.

Lost, lost, lost. The animals all knew it. The fishes of the sea would hear that strange music vibrate along the ocean bed, but the water would not carry it to the forest creatures. Never again would Glim know so clearly that part of him that was more than his everyday monkey-being.

All things now were moving backward. What the music

143

had drawn forth was returning to the shell of normal living. Glim went with the others, back to the things he knew so well.

Many creatures, like Marga, had heard nothing. But the disturbance had echoes and the echoes were picked up in discontentment. Marga's anger was terrible this time when Glim returned after such long absence. Her teeth were fully bared, her eyes wide, as if challenging him to approach if he dared. Yet woe betide him if he went elsewhere. Now, or in the future.

Time and tiredness and Uhu brought about a change. As night came they lay down together in weariness, ready for sleep to heal the rift. The new day would know nothing of the old.

While they slept the stars grew clearer above. At the bottom of deep waters, in the world of fish and frond, a stone shone like a star, its light striking up to the ruffling surface. As the waters grew still for a space the stone's light joined the reflection of the heavens.

Glim awoke while it was still night and the scents of the forest were strong around him. Marga's peaceful breathing spoke of her soothed spirits, that all was well. Yet something had woken Glim that was both strange and familiar. The blending of the two puzzled him the more and made him rub the creases between his eyes. He moved from Marga's side, stealing cautiously out from the tightly meshed branches and ascending the tree's thick foliage.

It was not Glim's habit to look at the sky, for his natural posture was groundward. Yet this time he was drawn to gaze upward. The heavens were aglow with a pure cold light and from every star came distant strains of sound that, mingling together, filled the firmament. The music swelled, a hundred times richer, fuller, than what had issued from the stone. It swept from constellations that Glim's eyes could not see nor his brain picture.

One thing he dimly understood. Here was a blessing and

144

a promise that could not be carried off or hidden or destroyed. Marga still might not hear it, but it was there. That glorious light was there and he could find it again, and listen again. And Marga too and Uhu might one day see and hear.

DRAGON-IN-LOVE

Jemmopholus, commonly known as Jemmy, was a dragon of the usual bulk and quick temper. He was remarkable only for a certain speed of movement which was unexpected in a dragon and had allowed him to get in many a wicked lash of his tail when he played with other young dragons while the old ones grunted and slept and rolled in the sun.

The frolicsome days were over, for Jemmy was a mature dragon now, with a breadth of chest of which he was truly proud. This was the first season he would choose his own cave for winter residence and select a mate from among the swarms of admiring females.

The dragons of this colony were lazy creatures, for hills and rocks had cut them off from many outside dangers. You couldn't take them for anything but what they were, earth-born and earth-grown, and staunch in their ways as generations before them. Their greatest pleasure was to roll in dust and sunshine. When the cold of winter came they took to the surrounding caves and found warmth in family life.

Now at the mating season it was usual for the fattest females to be chosen first. Since Jemmy was a handsome dragon there was a lot of competition for his attention. His family all expected him to choose the plumpest, glossiest female he could find. He was good enough, they said, for the great Gudrun herself. Then they laughed and belched with dragon humour, for Gudrun was no more than a legend, though a very *big* legend indeed. She was supposed to be the largest dragon that ever lived. It was said she could swallow three of her own kind and not be stretched in bulk. It was said she would devour the flesh of female

149

dragons for she hated rivals, but the male dragons she kept
as husbands and only sometimes added them to the food
pile when stocks got low.

So Jemmy was teased with the thought of Gudrun, but
he answered their teasing by doing a terrible thing. He fell
in love.

When Jemmy approached Lara she looked away from
him as if recognising that the other dragons would dis-
approve. For Lara was not considered an asset in the
dragon colony, being pale and thin and rather humble. Besides, dragons didn't fall in love. They were much too
practical, earth-born and earth-grown. Food and fat companions and sunny dust-patches were things they apprecia-
ted, but falling in love was beyond their understanding.

While Jemmy's mates laughed, the females became quite
cross to think that Jemmy should disregard such fine
creatures as themselves and sigh over silly little Lara. If his
attention had not been so fixed on her he might have
noticed sooner how dangerous things were becoming, how
jealous glinting eyes watched both him and the quiet Lara
into the heart of the night.

The thing about being in love, Jemmy discovered, was
that it made you see the world in a new way. Most of the
time you went through life thinking food and large caves
and shiny stones were important. But if you were in love
even the cold of winter wasn't something to make a fuss
about.

It was his family that woke Jemmy up rather sharply.

"Can't you see what's happening?" they said. "Why
can't you be like us?"

Jemmy was amazed that others should care what he was
doing. Provided they had good caves, good sun patches and
good females, they didn't usually mind if others got less
than the best. Now he found that his sighing over Lara
made the other dragons uneasy. They couldn't bear that he
should disregard their ways and not eat and not fight for a

cave. They resented him spending his time puffing little rings of smoke towards Lara. She herself never stirred to look in his direction. But Jemmy persisted and the more Lara ignored him the more he attended to her.

Things came to a head among the dragons. What had begun as a cause for laughter was now deeply irritating. Some of them began to puff frightfully at a mere glimpse of Jemmy, and all of them could find something in life to make them bad-tempered. Perhaps it was a stone one had swallowed, or a bit of rheumatism in the leg heralding bad weather, or grumpiness when daylight came too soon. Yet something had to be done to soothe ruffled tempers. It was obvious that Jemmy would have to go.

If he hadn't been quick-moving he would have received more of those painful slaps with scaly tails that the other dragons were always waving round him. Their great bodies would block his way and push him in any but the right direction. None of the caves, not even the smallest or most exposed, had been left for him. It needed only one quick spurt of anger before he was told:

"No more room. We're over-crowded on this side. You must cross the hills and search in the next valley for a cave."

Jemmy suddenly realised that he was being expelled. His family had turned against him. All the dragons wanted him to go. It was a dismal prospect, for the colony of dragons had never existed outside of this plot of secluded ground where the caves were theirs, the valley was theirs, the sun itself was theirs. Who could say what discomforts and what dangers lay among the hills?

Yet there was something stubborn in Jemmy that determined him to face the journey and to find a cave for himself. Later he would return and carry off Lara as his cave-companion.

It was a painful move, out through the rocks and towards the skyline, for the wind blew colder on the heights and winter was drawing in. Yet to Jemmy the greatest sorrow was leaving Lara behind. He must move quickly forward in order to accomplish his task the sooner.

He had almost forgotten that beyond the hills there could lie dangerous things that might be as much opposed to his love as his own dragon brood had been. Then one clear dawn he was suddenly impressed with strange cliffs, seemingly empty of life. One huge formation of rock rose like an organ loft above dark areas that could be cave-mouths. That magnificent range might hold all kinds of possible nook and cranny.

Jemmy knew that at this time of year caves might not be entirely empty and that he might be at risk in exploring them. Still he travelled on until massive protective rock towered above him, while beneath stretched the valley open to sun and sky. Nothing stirred except for the solitary eagles wheeling above.

Jemmy rushed forward, scenting first one cave, then another. The next one always drew him on, appearing more interesting than the last. The caves wound into and out of the sun, and Jemmy had no idea how far he had gone. He emerged into a sheltered spot which gave a good view of the valley below. The sun was striking the rock and it was giving out more heat than usual for the time of year. The winter could be short and the summer delightfully long among these cliffs. He moved forward to where the next black mouth gaped through jagged stone.

As he stepped into the cave he suddenly felt the onrush of foul air and a breath that lapped over his head and round his limbs and clouded his scales and turned his sto-mach. He moved sufficiently back into the sun to draw out the creature he'd encountered. Now he saw that the legend had not exaggerated but rather had forgotten to add foul-ness and horror to the description of Gudrun. The sight of her was enough to cause his limbs to ebb in strength.

Along Gudrun's great mouth and neck were signs of the

blood that had dripped both inside and out. The greater part of her body still lay within the cave, too hideous for the light of day. Her front feet encircled the luckless Jemmy and her tongue ran along the stretch of his back. Now he knew why these caves had all been empty of life. Behind Gudrun would lie bones in the blackness.

Jemmy gave a lurch and sought to free himself. Gudrun, however, was well-practised in dealing with her prey and could not be avoided so easily. For all Jemmy's breadth of chest he was no match for the monstrous she-dragon. For long minutes they wrestled, and Gudrun was tossing him backwards and forwards like a pebble.

Jemmy panted desperately. Then a thought came over him. What reason had he to care if this were his end? Who would weep if he were captured or devoured? He was an outcast now, and as an outcast he was losing the will to struggle.

Then his eye fell on the valley and the rocks. What a home it might have been for Lara and himself. There was a little plateau of rock at the other side of the valley, flat in the sun except for a shape that suddenly stood out to Jemmy's sight. Was it — could it be — a dragon lying motionless? Was that Lara looking towards him?

Jemmy's heart beat as if it would break its bounds. Had Lara followed him, or been cast out after his departure? He was convinced that she was waiting and watching while he wrestled. The shape now slipped from the plateau and out of Jemmy's view.

He found new strength in his contest with Gudrun. What vileness to be her husband and her slave. Better even to die in the struggle than yield to that!

Jemmy remembered the tricks he used to play as a young dragon. He had always beaten the other dragons by speedy movement. He let himself sink exhausted between Gudrun's huge feet. Her lips which had been pinching his skin relaxed their hold when she felt his resistance give way. With a great leap Jemmy shot from her clutch, whipping his sharp tail up across her eyes as he had been used to lash out in the sand-pits with his comrades. The tail caught Gudrun on the forehead, stinging both eyes into a blinding redness. She howled furiously and lashed out, but Jemmy's speed and her sudden blindness had secured his release. He was several yards now from the cave, on the other side of boulders, away from her dribbling jaws.

He sank exhausted, for the struggle had torn out several scales and his sides ached. Gudrun was still howling wildly, but she was unused to the light and retreating fast into her cave for protection. Had he simply foiled her hopes for the present time, or had he struck more fatally? Jemmy found he had no strength to drag himself further. In a little while, after he had rested, he would go in search of Lara. He lay in a deep swoon in the shadow of the boulders.

While he rested there was more noise in the valley. Jemmy lay for a long time unaware of what was happening. When he did rouse himself he was conscious both of his pain and also of the smell of enemy. A more famous destroyer of the dragon brood than Gudrun was at hand. So far, however, the knight had not seen Jemmy. He stood with stained sword close to Gudrun at the entrance to her cave. The great she-dragon was stretched on her side and bleeding.

Instinct was strong in Jemmy and it told him that here was new danger. Still, he could see only one of these human creatures before him. Dragging his aching limbs together, Jemmy rose, ready to do battle. The knight turned quickly and glimpsed him. His armour threw rays across Jemmy's eyes. Then noises at a distance told Jemmy that the knight was not alone. A lady's voice echoed from behind rocks, bidding the knight return.

The knight, however, answered the call, bidding the lady be still. Then he mounted his horse and faced towards Jemmy. The plates of his armour were dancing like little suns. Jemmy gave the battle-cry and charged.

The knight's horse had been trained for such an event. It moved with a leap away from Jemmy's assault. The knight leaned to one side with lance poised. Jemmy was quick, but the lance caught his tail and drew blood. Jemmy's temper rose. He rushed again at the knight, using his great wing-span to stop the horse from avoiding him this time. The magnificent creature reared, lashed at one wing, causing a tendon to snap. Its rider, however, was down on the ground, secured by his heavy armour.

There was another shriek from the lady, disturbing Jemmy. He glanced in the direction of the rocks. The pause was long enough to allow the knight to get to his feet and secure a good position. He drew his sword.

Jemmy moved again to the attack. Now the knight was raising his sword against him, knowing that everything would depend on this blow. He gauged the part at the top of Jemmy's chest where the scales on the neck were scantier than on the rest of the body. The sword struck — very near — near enough to penetrate beneath the scaly frame and draw more blood. But the knight himself was overcome by the dragon's weight. Jemmy fell but in falling he pinned the knight to the ground by the leg. The dragon was badly wounded but he was not dead. The next blow would be Jemmy's.

Then came the lady's voice again, calling her lord, ringing through the valley. She was coming near. If her lord perished she would perish too. Jemmy dimly caught sight of her as she approached and a memory of Lara swept over him; somewhere at hand she would be waiting. He raised himself with an effort, releasing the knight who expected that Jemmy's move signalled he was about to strike.

But Jemmy struck no blow. Instead he let his head sink against the rock and surrendered to his wounds. The blood flowed from many gashes, the scales lay broken and the limbs motionless.

155

When night came Jemmy's huge frame lay alone in silence on the rocky ground. The valley was open to the heavens, peaceful now and silent. Gudrun, who had ruled there, would rule no more.

With the night came Lara. With the moon and the stars she moved slowly through the valley. With the starlight she found Jemmy on his patch of stony ground. With the moon she stretched out beside him.

Moon and stars and cave and sky watched Lara as she lay all night licking Jemmy's wounds. The blood had darkened his scales and the dust had roughened them, but Lara stretched close beside him and licked him clean, performing her task with a patience like the sad slow patience of the moon.

Then with the dawn Jemmy stirred.